"You!"

Hannah's word c
she had no time
stepped forward
forward hard onto the floor.

It seemed to happen in slow motion.

Noah reached her first and helped her to her feet.

"Denki." Hannah knew the word had come out stiffly, but she was fortunate that she had managed to speak at all. Noah's proximity had set her heart racing, and vibrations were running through her. She felt as though she had placed her hand on a generator. Her breath came in short bursts.

"I'm fine. I'm fine," Hannah protested. "I'm just *doplich*."

"You're not clumsy, Hannah. Are you hurt?"

"Nee."

Only my heart is hurt, Hannah thought.

Why did her heart race so when she saw him?

How could her feelings for him still be there after everything Noah Hostetler had done to her, and not only to her, but to her sisters, too?

Ruth Hartzler is an internationally bestselling and award-winning author of clean and sweet romance, mystery, and suspense, including Amish romance, Christian romance and Christian cozy mysteries. Ruth is the recipient of several All-Star Awards (author and book).

THE WAY HOME

Ruth Hartzler

ISBN-13: 978-1-335-49967-7

The Way Home

This edition published by arrangement with Harlequin Books S.A.

For questions and comments about the quality of this book, please contact us at CustomerService@Harlequin.com.

Printed in U.S.A.

Chapter One

Hannah smoothed down her dark plain-cut dress and looked out the window of the buggy, admiring the shimmering frost and the ribbons of silver mist. It was early morning in the wintertime, and the Miller sisters had only just stepped into their *familye's* buggy. They were going to visit with their friends on the other side of their town. Hannah was the oldest, the wisest, and the one everyone thought of as sensible, dutiful, and kind. Like her three younger sisters, she wore a heavy bonnet over her prayer *kapp* this morning, although she had not worn her long woolen cloak.

Sitting by her older *schweschder*, Esther pulled distractedly on the corner of her cloak; she had not braved the cold like Hannah. Esther was the second oldest of the Millers. Unlike the two youngest *schweschders*, Martha and Rebecca, Esther sat in complete silence this morning. Hannah wondered if Esther was thinking on next Sunday's Singing, but she felt a little too sleepy to ask just yet. She would wait another five minutes or so. Besides, on the other side of the buggy, Martha and Rebecca were chatting about their chores, and Hannah thought it pleasant to listen to the sweet, low chime of their voices. *Familye* was so important to her, and she cherished every minute with Esther, Martha, and Rebecca.

On the other side of town, Noah Hostetler pulled on his leather jacket and stepped out of his family's *haus*. He loved the smell of winter, the wood smoke and the frost. For a moment, he stood in the cooling air next to the ancient rust bucket he called a car, borrowed from one his *Englisch* friends. He would never admit this to his younger *bruders*, but he loved how pleasant and quiet the world was this early in the morning. After a sigh, he slipped into the driver's seat and started the engine.

Noah was on *rumspringa*, so he could dress *Englisch* and drive vehicles other than ones drawn by horses. Checking to make sure his side-view mirrors were properly adjusted, he lurched down the driveway toward the center of town. The road was icy, and the mist pressed into his car, so he was careful not to drive too fast.

Back in the Millers' buggy, Esther took a deep breath, and then sighed. "We should get a lot of sewing done this coming winter. I want to make another bonnet each for Martha and Rebecca," she whispered to Hannah. "I'd like to make another shirt for *daed*, too."

"I think that's a *gut* idea," Hannah replied. "Esther, is anything troubling you? You seem a little quiet this morning." Esther was more reserved than her three sisters, but she usually spoke more than this.

"I was thinking about seeing Jacob," she replied in a low voice, "next Sunday at the Singing." Hannah and Esther never spoke loudly about boys around Martha and Rebecca, because they could not risk their younger *schweschders* overhearing. The relentless teasing that would follow would be too embarrassing, so they talked only to each other about courting.

Noah rolled down the window. The windshield was almost too foggy to see through. He hoped that letting in a rush of cold air would clear up the glass, and he smiled to himself with relief when the winding road in front of his car became a little bit more visible. Light was spilling over the horizon now, painting the wintry landscape in hues of yellow, pink, and purple, and it was almost worth the dangerous driving conditions for the beauty of the scenery.

"What are you two whispering about?" Martha said, reaching out to pinch Esther's hand. She had stopped talking with Rebecca in order to take a keen interest in the conversation of her older *schweschders*. "Are you talking about boys?"

"You are." Rebecca wagged her finger at Hannah and Esther. "Come on; we're sisters. You're not meant to keep anything from us, remember? We made a deal."

Hannah chuckled. "I don't recall making any sort of deal." Despite herself, she couldn't help but smile at her two youngest *schweschders*. "You two had best leave Esther alone. Look, the sun's finally up," she said, pointing to the golden light spilling over the white hills. The diversion tactic worked, because all four Miller sisters stopped talking to admire the scenery.

Noah tightly grasped the steering wheel. The road was slippery this morning, and in this part of town, where the great trees threw deep shadows over the road, he could hardly see a thing in front of him. Despite his best efforts, the window had also fogged up once more. For a moment, he even considered pulling the car over and waiting ten minutes until the driving conditions had improved. If only he had.

"Where did the sun go?" Rebecca asked, pushing her nose against the window of the buggy. "It looked so pretty through the mist and against the frost."

"This part of town is full of trees, remember?" said Esther, gently. "I imagine they're doing a good job of blocking out the sun. Don't worry about it too much."

Rebecca fidgeted in her seat. "I can't wait to get there."

"Me too," added Martha.

"I expect it won't be too much longer," Hannah assured them. "I'm so looking forward to…"

For a moment time froze, and then a great, shattering bang broke the winter hush. Hannah later remembered her head colliding with the wall of the buggy, her younger sisters screaming as all four of them were flung into the air, and the sickening silence that followed. She remembered lying on the frost-covered ground and wishing for her heavy woolen coat. She remembered a sharp pain throbbing through her leg, while she wondered how she had escaped the overturned buggy. Lastly, she remembered a young man crawling out of his overturned car and moving toward her through the ribbons of silver mist, to see if she was still breathing.

Chapter Two

2 Months Later

Hannah rested on her crutches for a moment and looked at the clouds gathering in the late winter sky. She held her face skyward, letting the icy breeze flow across her face. Winter wrens flew overhead. *They have no cares*, Hannah thought, *just like I once had no cares or worries.*

Before the accident, Hannah had led a carefree life, surrounded by the love of her *familye* and the closeness of her community. The accident had changed all that.

Hannah had thought she would marry Noah. She had been so certain. She had mapped out their whole life—their babies growing up, playing in the dirt between the vegetables and the colorful flowers in the kitchen garden. She could almost smell the jasmine in her imagined garden now. Hannah's mother frowned upon flowers with no purpose, but Hannah knew jasmine had antiseptic properties. It had its place amongst comfrey, feverfew, horehound, and yarrow.

In her mind's eye, Hannah saw her *bopplin* growing into fine, upstanding *kinner*, but then she caught herself and came back to the harsh light of reality. She had been certain she and Noah would grow old together, watching their grandchildren come along, and maybe even their great-grandchildren, if it was *Gott's* will. The possibility that it could be otherwise had not once crossed her mind. And yet it was different now. The accident had changed all that.

Her *familye's* retired buggy horse, Rock, broke across her thoughts, softly nickering to her from his pasture. "I'm not feeding you any oats, Rock," she scolded him. "Every time I appear, you think I'm going to feed you. You're retired now, and you have plenty of hay to eat."

Hannah noticed Rock's thick winter blanket was slipping somewhat to one side. "Don't worry, Rock," she said. "I'll tell *Datt* and he'll straighten it. If I tried, I would overbalance and hurt myself."

Rock lost interest in Hannah when he saw she wasn't going to feed him, and wandered away. Hannah watched him closely, the wind lifting the wooly hair on his long neck, contrasting with the smooth, glossy coat under his blankets.

She was relieved that Rock was no longer lame. The veterinarian hadn't held out much hope for Rock after the accident, but with old Mrs. Graber's comfrey liniments and poultices, he was now walking sound. Still, he would never pull a buggy again.

Hannah hobbled her way back to her *haus* as best she could with her crutches and heavy cast, thinking Rock was doing better than she was. Mrs. Graber had helped her somewhat, but Rock could now walk normally, whereas it would be a while before she could. And of course, Mrs. Graber's comfrey liniments could not heal a broken heart.

"Hannah, Hannah!" Esther's voice broke through her thoughts.

Hannah turned sharply, losing one crutch as she did so. She grabbed it and managed to regain her footing before she fell. After she carefully retrieved the crutch from the ground, she hobbled back to the *haus*.

The steps to the porch always gave her trouble, although by now she'd had plenty of practice.

As Hannah opened the door, a blast of warm air hit her in the face. She heard her *mudder's* scolding words, "Hush, Esther. Why do you keep calling for Hannah?"

"Sorry, *Mamm*, but you told me not to call you anymore and I need a glass of water. I did try not to call, but my throat's so parched and dry that I couldn't wait any longer."

Hannah hurried into the room and looked at her *mudder*, whom she figured was even wearier than she. "I'll get it, *Mamm*."

Her *mudder* smiled at her oldest *dochder. "Denki."*

Hannah had to stifle feelings of resentment

against her sisters. She was injured too, and the *doktor* had told her to stay off her leg as much as possible. Unfortunately for Hannah, her *doktor* didn't realize just how demanding her sisters would be. Not that it was their fault, but that fact didn't make it any easier or her load any lighter.

Hannah allowed herself a small sigh. "I'm coming, Esther."

All the girls' bedrooms were upstairs, but after the accident, Mr. Miller put mattresses downstairs so that the girls could be looked after more easily. It was also warmer downstairs, near the potbelly stove in the living room. Hannah was on crutches and unable to get up the stairs anyway, and it was easier all round if the three injured girls were together downstairs. The girls were on mattresses across the floor of the living room, around the potbelly stove. It was a blessing that the bathroom was downstairs also.

"Me too please, Hannah," Martha said with a cough.

"All right. It'll take me a minute." Hannah wondered how she was going to carry the water back, without having both her hands on the crutches. At that moment she remembered the tray-mobile their elderly *grossmammi* used to wheel around in the *haus*. She was sure it was still in the storeroom off from the kitchen.

Hannah moved with her crutches the best she could and opened the storeroom door. Yes, just as she thought, the tray-mobile was there. Now all she had to do was move the sack of sugar from on top of it and she would have the answer to her problem. Well, an answer to one of her problems.

As she filled two glasses with water after struggling with the sugar sack, she wondered how Rebecca was getting on. The only way she could find out was to call the hospital herself from the phone in the barn.

After Hannah gave her sisters a glass of water each, she hobbled back to the front door. The air had a decidedly chilly cast after leaving the sanctuary of the warm house. Hannah slowly headed for the phone in the barn to make the call to the hospital. She was getting better on the crutches, but still found it difficult to maneuver stairs. There were only five steps down from the porch, but it felt more like fifty.

She was relieved that she didn't have to drive to the nearest shanty to make the call. The accident had left Hannah afraid of buggies, and the nearest shanty was several farms away. The bishop had given Hannah's father permission to install a phone in the barn given that he conducted his business on the property.

Hannah stood for a moment, letting the warmth of the barn sink in. She was cold, although figured most of it was from weariness. It was tiresome having to hobble everywhere with her leg in a heavy cast. It was also difficult having to care for others when she was far from recovery.

Still, everyone had burdens. Hannah shook herself and called the hospital.

The hospital transferred her call to Rebecca's room. "How are you?"

"Hannah!" Rebecca's voice was filled with delight. "A little better, and it doesn't hurt so much when I move my legs now."

Hannah could sense from her *schweschder's* voice that something was troubling her. "Yes, *Mamm* told me, but are you sure you're all right?"

"Jah."

Hannah heard a couple sniffs on the other end of the phone.

"Hannah, you're going to come see me today, aren't you? You didn't come yesterday." Rebecca's voice was small and sad.

Hannah turned her eyes to the roof. How could she possibly get to the hospital every single day? She never wanted to go in a buggy ever again; they were far too dangerous, and so she had to take a taxi every time she visited Rebecca. She sighed and then caught herself. "Of course I am," she said in the most cheerful voice she could muster.

Buggies were not the only things that filled Hannah with horror. Now she was wondering how she could continue to set foot inside the hospital day after day. Every time she hobbled on the crutches to the front door of the hospital, dread filled her. The antiseptic smell of the hospital made her want to turn and run. Worse still, there were buggies in the parking area, and buggies made her want to run away, to the point of bringing on an anxiety attack. She always found it hard to breathe and had to take a few long, slow breaths.

Hannah was the one who most visited Rebecca.

Her *daed* was busy with his woodworking business, and her *mudder* was busy with all the chores and doing the cooking by herself, now that the three *schweschders* who were at home could not do much if anything at all.

Hannah talked with Rebecca a little longer until she was sure that her younger sister was much happier. Hannah rested her elbows on her crutches and called the number for the taxi. That was the only possible way for her to get there. She felt guilty that her parents had to spend money on taxis, but there was no way she would ever go near a buggy again, let alone actually get into one or drive one.

Chapter Three

The automatic doors of the hospital opened. Hannah hesitated at the entrance as people jostled to pass her from either side.

After a moment, Hannah sensed someone standing beside her. She looked up to see a handsome man in a suit.

"Can I help you, miss? Are you all right?"

Hannah guessed that he was a doctor as he had the very same self-important air about him as the doctor who had been treating her. "I'm fine, *denki*." Hannah continued to stand in the entrance while she summoned the courage to walk through the doors.

The man was still standing beside her when he said, "You're kind of blocking the doorway."

Hannah looked at him. He had kind, soft brown eyes and he was smiling at her.

"Oh, I'm so sorry. I didn't mean to." She took a quick step back in an effort to move from the doorway, and overbalanced.

The young man quickly stepped behind her and steadied her with strong hands. "There you go," he said, as she regained her balance.

"Thank you." Hannah wanted to adjust her bonnet over her prayer *kapp* as she was sure it was now tilted a little, but she dared not take her hands off her crutches.

"Are you sure you don't need any help? Are you here as a patient, or are you visiting someone?"

"Visiting someone."

"Aha." The young man nodded his head. "Well, let's just step through here and we'll see if we can find their room number, shall we?"

He took a step as if he expected Hannah to step with him, but Hannah could not move.

"Is there anything wrong? Are you having trouble with your crutches?"

Hannah was aware heat rose to her cheeks. Did she have to explain herself and her fears to someone she didn't know? Since he looked as though he were a doctor and was obviously a thoughtful and caring person, Hannah decided to trust him. "It's just that I'm a little afraid."

The young man put his head to one side. "Afraid of…?"

"Going in there." She nodded her head toward the hospital.

"I see. And who is it that you've come to see?"

"My sister, her name's Rebecca. We were in a buggy accident together. I was in the hospital for a while, but she's still here. I do know her room number as I visit her most days."

He scratched his chin. "Well, speaking as a doctor, I would advise you not to visit your sister."

Hannah was aghast. "Don't visit her?" she exclaimed. "But she's waiting for me; I told her I'd come. I come nearly every day. It's just that..." Hannah's voice trailed away.

"Aren't you scared, though?"

Hannah looked up at the hospital and then back at the doctor. "Yes, but I have to go in."

The doctor looked at Hannah for a moment before he said, "What if I take you in the back way? You can pretend that you're walking into a different building and not into a hospital."

Hannah nodded. "That would be good."

The doctor smiled and said, "This way." He took Hannah around the side of the large building and through an insignificant-looking door. Hannah forced herself to pretend that she was just going into any old building and not into a hospital.

"There, we're in." The doctor smiled at Hannah, revealing a perfect set of teeth. "I'm Dr. Hanson."

"It's nice to meet you. Thank you for helping me. My name's Hannah Miller."

"Would you like me to call for a nurse to help you to your sister's room?"

Hannah shook her head. "*Nee*, I'm sure I've taken up enough of your time already."

He smiled again and tipped his head. "Glad to be of service."

Hannah took a firm hold of her crutches and made her way to her sister's room. *Breathe, Hannah, breathe*, she told herself. She found that breathing deeply, and turning her attention away from what was troubling her, always helped her greatly.

Noah Hostetler was leaving the hospital after visiting Rebecca, and saw Hannah walk around the side of the building with a handsome young *mann*. The *mann* had his hand on Hannah's arm, helping her along on her crutches, the crutches that he, Noah, was responsible for. A sharp pang of guilt struck at Noah's heart, followed closely by a pang of jealousy.

"Hannah!" Rebecca let out a squeal of delight when she saw Hannah, and Hannah at once felt bad for not having wanted to come. It wasn't that she didn't want to visit Rebecca—she did, but it was the hospital that made her afraid.

Hannah still remembered vividly how she had awoken in a cold, sterile room and the first thing that she had been able to remember was the faint yet unpleasant smell of the hospital disinfectant. She also remembered the unbearable pain in her leg and how much her head hurt. She remembered the fear of not knowing what had happened to her sisters.

Finally, her parents had been allowed into her room and explained that she had broken her leg, and that Martha had two broken ankles and a broken arm. They told her that Esther and Rebecca both had a spinal injury in the form of a herniated disc.

However, Martha was now at home as her back injury had responded to medication, whereas Rebecca's back injury was far worse and had required surgery.

Hannah felt yet another pang of anger toward Noah Hostetler. They had known each other since childhood, and never would she have imagined that he would turn out to be so irresponsible, even on his *rumspringa.* It was only through the grace of *Gott* that no one had been killed by Noah's reckless driving. Even poor old Rock, the big bay Saddlebred gelding that had always pulled the family wagon, was now retired due to leg injuries sustained in the accident.

Hannah drew her attention back to Rebecca. *Oh well, we're all alive, and even Rock is too*, she thought. Still, she could not get rid of the bitterness in her heart toward Noah. She even used to have tender feelings for him, before the accident of course. Now, her only feelings for him were of anger and resentment.

Back then, Hannah had thought that she would one day marry Noah, but that was before he went on *rumspringa.* That had filled her with dismay. Hannah herself had never even wanted to go on *rumspringa.* The ways of the *Englisch* held no attraction for her, none whatsoever. Now her former adoration for Noah had faded, not surprisingly since he was the cause of all their injuries.

"Hannah! You seem a million miles away."

Hannah jumped. "Sorry. I was lost in thought,"

she said, as she sat on the end of Rebecca's bed. Hannah would be happy if she never sat on a hospital bed again. She forced her thoughts away from focusing on herself. "How are you feeling today? I'm sorry I haven't come to see you sooner."

Rebecca smiled. "I'm okay. Are you okay? I know the hospital really frightens you. Anyway, I'm very glad you've come to visit. I don't know what I'd do without my big sister."

Hannah reached out to clasp her hand. "I'll always be here for you," she said, as Rebecca stifled a yawn. "Are you tired?"

"I am, but don't think you're going to get away with avoiding the subject. Tell me what you were thinking about. Don't make me guess. You know how annoying I can be when I'm trying to guess what's on your mind."

Hannah laughed heartily. "No matter what's going on, you always guess that the problem's a boy."

Rebecca chuckled. "And I'm always right. So are you going to talk about Noah Hostetler, or are you going to spend this whole visit thinking about him while I sit here staring at you? I'm fine with either." Rebecca smirked at her.

Hannah scrunched up her nose. She had no wish to speak about Noah Hostetler, but did not want Rebecca to know how she now felt about him. After all, Rebecca had shown no sign at all that she resented Noah for the accident. "Would you tease me relentlessly if I did talk to you about a boy?"

"Absolutely," Rebecca said, "but you still have

to tell me. Don't make me go on and on about how bad I feel, until you have to confess everything out of pity for me. So, do you still like Noah, or not?"

Hannah sighed deeply. "He just seems so changed," she said. "*Rumspringa* has turned him into a person I no longer recognize. I did have feelings for him, I truly did. I know we can never marry now. Not after what happened."

Rebecca shook her head. "Don't take this to heart, but aren't you being a little too harsh on Noah? We've known the Hostetler family our entire lives. There's nobody kinder or more generous."

Hannah shrugged. *If only I could be as forgiving as Rebecca*, she thought. Aloud she said, "I suppose."

"Besides, the accident wasn't really Noah's fault," Rebecca said. "They say he was a careful driver, but you remember how misty it was that morning? How frosty the roads were? We could hardly see a thing." Rebecca stifled another yawn. "Sorry, Hannah. I'm excited to see you. I'm just more tired than I thought."

Hannah stood up and patted her *schweschder* on the shoulder. "You rest," she said. "I promise to visit again tomorrow. No matter how terrified I am of hospitals, I'd never dream of letting down my youngest sister."

Chapter Four

That night, there was great excitement in the Miller *haus* as it was the first time that the three sisters who were back at home were able to sit at the table to eat dinner. Martha had to be helped from the wheelchair onto a chair, as the table was too high for her. Her legs were healing well, but as both had been broken, she was unable to hop along like Hannah could. She was getting better at eating with her left hand, but still had to have all her food cut up for her.

Martha often said she wished it had been her left arm that had been broken, rather than her right. Mrs. Miller always responded somewhat sharply that it would be better if neither had been broken.

Mrs. Miller, with Hannah's help, had prepared meatloaf and mashed potatoes. This was also the first time that the girls' physical therapist, Amy Nolt, had accepted Mrs. Miller's invitation to stay for dinner after one of her visits.

Mrs. Nolt was an *Englischer*, and had vivid purple hair the color of dark grape juice. What's more, it was short. Hannah knew her mother did not approve, and had overheard her muttering various things about women who cut their hair or made it into a color that *Gott* had never intended for them, or for anyone's hair for that matter.

On the other hand, Hannah was fascinated by Amy Nolt. Apart from various doctors, Mrs. Nolt was the *Englischer* with whom Hannah had the closest contact. Hannah would have loved to ask her how she had made her hair that color, but didn't think it appropriate. Still, no matter what color hair Mrs. Nolt sported, she was a caring and expert physical therapist and Hannah was certain she was responsible for how far she had progressed. That, and Mrs. Graber's potions.

"How did your hair turn purple?" Rebecca asked Amy. "My parents both have brown hair, but *Mamm's* eyes are brown like yours whereas *Datt's* eyes are blue. Hannah and I have brown eyes, but Esther and Martha have blue eyes. We all have brown hair, though, although Martha's has a red tone and Hannah's is more fair."

"Hush with your chatter, child," Mrs. Miller rebuked her. "Mrs. Nolt can see for herself what color eyes you have, and it is rude to comment on her hair. Apologize at once."

Rebecca lowered her eyes. "I'm sorry."

"That's fine, truly," Amy said. "I don't mind at all."

Mrs. Miller looked at her *dochders*. "Thank *Der Herr* you're all recovering." She had a tear in her eye.

Hannah was concerned to see her *mudder's* face, considering Mrs. Miller had never really shown any outward affection.

"My back hurts a bit though, *Mamm*," Esther said, "but it's much better than lying on my side to eat. This is *gut*, being able to sit up."

"Don't sit for too long then, Esther," Amy said. "Go lie down if it hurts too much. You shouldn't overdo it. If it gets worse, it will be a long time before you'll be able to sit again."

Esther nodded and ate another mouthful of mashed potato.

Amy Nolt made a sound of appreciation. "I must say, Mrs. Miller, these are the best mashed potatoes I've ever tasted. What's in them?"

Hannah thought her mother appeared embarrassed. Praise was not freely given within Amish communities.

Mrs. Miller flushed beet red. "Um, eggs, butter, salt, sugar, yeast." She turned to her husband. "How was your work today?"

Mr. Miller looked down at his food. Hannah wondered if he was hiding something, but then dismissed the idea as fanciful. After all, what on earth could her *daed* be hiding?

"Gut." Her usually talkative *daed* had still not looked up, and Hannah was sure that her *mudder* was glaring at him.

Amy Bolt appeared oblivious to the sudden tension. "What work do you do, Mr. Miller? Farming?"

Mr. Miller did look up then, and his face relaxed

into a smile. "*Nee*, Mrs. Nolt. I used to, but with four girls I decided to scale down the farming and start another business some years ago. I'm a woodworker; I have a furniture store."

Amy Nolt looked interested. "What kind of furniture do you make?"

"Many things. We make cedar bedroom sets—oak ones too—mailboxes, birdhouses, and all sorts of furniture really, from oak, cherry, hickory, and cedar. Rocking chairs are most likely our best sellers."

Amy Nolt nodded. "Oh yes, I know your store. I've been in there a few times. My husband loves the craftsmanship."

There was silence for a while, until Mrs. Miller left the table to fetch the blueberry pie.

"Hannah."

"Yes, *Datt*?" Hannah looked up to see her *daed's* blue eyes twinkling mischievously at her.

"I was speaking to Mr. Hostetler today and he tells me that Mrs. Hostetler could do with some help with sewing quilts."

It took Hannah a moment to realize that her *daed* wanted her to help Mrs. Hostetler. "But, *Datt*," she protested, "I'm not *piffling* around here. My days are already taken up by helping Hannah and Martha and trying to help *Mamm*, and visiting Rebecca in the hospital!"

Mr. Miller fixed her with a stern look of disapproval. "The pay is *gut*."

Hannah immediately was ashamed. The medical expenses for her and her sisters were high, and her parents had refused financial help from the Hostetlers. Her parents had, of course, accepted the free-will plan, where their community had taken up an offering, and then their community had sent to neighboring communities to take up an offering. Still, it was not enough to cover all the expenses. The community had also raised funds through food drives. While no one had discussed it openly with her, Hannah had gotten the impression that while these had gone a considerable way to paying the expenses, there was still a significant shortfall.

Hannah suspected that the Hostetlers had contributed heavily to the free-will plan, but perhaps this was a way the Hostetlers figured they could contribute even more directly, by paying her wages for sewing. But where would she find the time? She was already exhausted. "Of course I will, *Datt.* I'd be happy to," she said as convincingly as she could. What choice did she have?

Mr. Miller beamed at her, but at that moment Mrs. Miller came back in with the blueberry pie. "Mrs. Hostetler," she muttered angrily to herself.

Hannah was glad that Amy Nolt was there, or further words would likely have been said.

"For if ye forgive men their trespasses, your heavenly Father will also forgive you. But if ye forgive not men their trespasses, neither will your Father forgive your trespasses," Mr. Miller said, his tone firm. Her *daed* always quoted the Bible to end arguments or to make his point.

Mrs. Miller did not respond, but muttered "Scripture smart" to herself, and cut into the blueberry pie with firmer than necessary strokes.

Amy leaned across the table. "Did you say 'Scripture smart'? Do you mind me asking what that means?"

Hannah held her breath. She wondered if the question would anger her *mudder.*

Still, Mrs. Miller did not appear to mind. "We believe that quoting Scripture is showing off," she said, fixing her husband with a glare.

Mr. Miller merely ate some meatloaf. Amy Nolt fidgeted in her seat, clearly realizing she had gotten Mr. Miller into trouble with her question.

Hannah's thoughts turned to her father's request. On this instance she agreed with her *mudder*—she wanted nothing to do with the Hostetler *familye*, but then again, her *familye* needed the money. What if she ran into Noah? *Nee*, surely Mrs. Hostetler would have the good sense to make sure that would never happen.

"Mrs. Hostetler's store is only one block from the hospital," Mr. Miller added, avoiding his wife's gaze, "so it won't take up any extra taxi money."

Both Esther and Martha shot Hannah sympathetic glances.

Hannah swallowed a mouthful of blueberries. *"Gut." Great,* she thought, *now I feel doubly guilty, all the medical bills and with me using money for taxis, just because I can't get over my fear of buggies*. She had suddenly lost her appetite.

Amy Nolt left soon after dinner, and Hannah did

her best to help her *mudder* in the kitchen. Esther's back was a little sore so Hannah filled a hot water bottle and set it in the small of her sister's back. She returned to the kitchen to fill a hot water bottle for Martha and one for herself. This took some doing, as she was only able to manage one at a time with her crutches. Hot water bottles all done, Hannah managed to get Martha out of her wheelchair and onto the mattress. Then she helped both girls into their thick flannel nightgowns.

Hannah opened the potbelly stove door and looked inside. It was almost out of wood. Hannah sighed. The potbelly was great for putting out warmth but it tended to go through too much wood too quickly. The little wood box nearby was empty, so Hannah hobbled out to the kitchen to ask her *daed* to fetch more wood from the wood box on the porch.

As she drew close, she heard her *daed's* voice. "Rachel, *was mer net weess macht eem net heess.*" *What you don't know won't hurt you.*

"*Nee*, Abraham. You must tell her! What happens when she finds out?" Mrs. Miller's voice was insistent.

Hannah hobbled forward on her crutches, wondering if they were talking about her, and at the same time, determined not to eavesdrop.

Her parents both looked at her, startled, and exchanged glances with each other. By their expressions, Hannah was left in no doubt that they *had* been talking about her. "*Mamm*, *Datt*, there's no wood inside for the potbelly stove."

Her *daed* jumped to his feet. "I'll get some now."

Mr. Miller carried wood inside and filled the pot-belly stove. He returned with more wood and stacked the wood box. "Are all you girls warm enough?"

"Jah, denki, Datt," they all said.

"Guten nacht."

"Good night, *Datt.*"

Mr. Miller scurried upstairs. Their *mudder* was still in the kitchen, banging pots around. Clearly, she was annoyed.

Hannah changed into her warm nightdress and climbed under the thick blankets that covered her mattress. She generally found warmth comforting. In fact, she normally found the sound of the cold wind outside soothing and the smell of the wood fires cheering, but tonight there was no reassurance to be found.

What were her parents keeping from her?

And why did her *mudder* want her to know about this mysterious matter, while her *daed* did not?

Chapter Five

Mrs. Miller looked up from her dusting. "Hannah, help me in the kitchen. We have guests coming for dinner."

The hairs stood up on the back of Hannah's neck. She hoped this was not another one of her mother's matchmaking attempts. "Who is it, *Mamm*?"

Her mother waved the feather duster at her. "The bishop has decided that we need more help around here, what with all you girls being injured. He has decided to send along a girl to help you all. She is going to stay in the *grossmammi haus*."

"What, she's coming tonight?" Hannah said in horror. "No one has lived in the *grossmammi haus* for years! There will be no time to clean it if she's coming tonight." Hannah took a firm hold on her crutches.

Mrs. Miller narrowed her eyes. "She and her *bruder* are staying with the Fischers until we get the *grossmammi haus* ready for her. I'm sure between the two of us we will have it looking spick-and-span in no time."

Hannah only just resisted the urge to groan. As if she didn't have enough duties, and now she would have to clean the *grossmammi haus* while on crutches. Still, it was very nice of the bishop to send someone to help them, and Hannah would certainly welcome the help. She silently chided herself for her unkind thoughts.

"Who is this girl who is coming? Do you know anything about her?"

Her mother shrugged one shoulder. "What does it matter, so long as she is a hard worker? I only know she's from another community and the bishop is friends with her father. Her *bruder* is accompanying her, and I've heard he's a fine young man." She emphasized the last few words.

Hannah took a deep breath. There it was, the matchmaking attempt she knew was coming. She was sure her mother already had her married off to this man and with a house full of *bopplin*—nothing surer. Perhaps her mother had given up trying to match her with David Yoder. David was the son of Mrs. Miller's close friend, Beth Yoder, and Mrs. Miller had made no secret that she wanted David and Hannah to marry. If her mother had, in fact, given up the idea of matching her with David, Hannah sure hoped her mother didn't think of this man as a backup.

"How old is he, *Mamm*?" Hannah asked, hoping he was not around her own age. If he was a much older man, then she would be wrong about her mother's trying to matchmake her with him.

Her spirits soon sank.

"Why, he is only five years older than you, Hannah. He is a farmer and makes enough money to support a house full of *bobblin*."

Hannah did groan aloud at that. It was just as she suspected.

"Don't give me that look, Hannah. I'm sure the two of you will become fast friends. Now hurry about, help me prepare the supper."

"What would you like me to do, *Mamm*?"

"We'll have two desserts tonight. I've already made the vanilla cornstarch pudding, so you can make a layered pudding with Jell-O and fruit. That's easy for you to do sitting down. I also made a banana pudding."

Hannah smiled to herself. A girl in the community had returned from *rumspringa* and told everyone that the *Englisch* only have one dessert at a meal.

Mrs. Miller was talking to herself, as she often did in the kitchen. Hannah figured it was her *mudder's* way of keeping organized. "*Jah*, the chicken's cooked. The potatoes, celery, and carrots are cooked. Now I'll just add the noodles. Hmm, that's the last thing to do. They can simmer for twenty-five minutes."

Hannah had only just put the layered dessert in the gas refrigerator when she heard her father's voice at the front door. She bit her lip. She hoped her mother's attempts to matchmake her with David would not be as obvious as they had been in the past, always leaving Hannah horribly embarrassed.

Hannah wiped her hands on a towel and reluctantly hobbled into the living room. The first thing she noticed was that the woman and man standing there were smiling widely. She took an instant liking to them both.

"John and Mary, this is my wife, Rachel Miller, and these are my *dochders*, Hannah, Esther, Martha, and Rebecca. Everyone, this is Mary and her brother, John Beiler."

Mrs. Miller hurried over to Mary. "I'm so glad you could come and help us," she said. "But I'm surprised you're not married by now."

The poor girl's face flushed beet red, and Hannah's heart went out to her.

"Um, um, no. Well, I suppose that means I'm free to come here and help you," she stammered. "It's not like I don't want to be married. I thought I'd be married by now too, and with *kinner*, but I'm not, as you can see."

Hannah noticed that John elbowed Mary lightly in the ribs, and figured it was to stop her talking.

"And it was good of you to accompany your *schweschder*," Mrs. Miller said to John.

"It was no trouble at all," he said. "I was happy to oblige."

"So, do you have a *fraa* at home?" Mrs. Miller asked John.

Hannah wished the ground would open up and swallow her. She heard her father's sharp intake of breath, and she exchanged a look with Esther. Of course her *mudder* knew the man was unmarried, for his face was cleanly shaven with not so much as full day's growth. All Amish married men grew beards from the day of their marriage. Hannah figured her mother was trying to find out if he was spoken for.

"No, I am not married, and I am not betrothed either," he said with a grin.

"I wonder why that is?" Mrs. Miller said, whether to herself or to John, Hannah did not know.

John patted his ample waistline. "I think the girls in my community require men with a finer figure than mine."

"Nonsense!" Mrs. Miller said. "I'm sure the girls in your community would not be so shallow. Come inside and get warm. I will fetch you a nice cup of meadow tea and we can all get acquainted before dinner."

Hannah was pleasantly relieved about John and Mary. They were friendly and outgoing enough, although Mary did seem a little shy, despite talking non-stop about anything and everything. John and Mary told the Millers about their community, which sounded quite pleasant.

"I hope you'll enjoy staying with us," Hannah said to Mary in a quiet voice when both her parents and John were engaged in conversation.

"I'm sure I will," she said shyly. "You all seem very nice. I was afraid to come here at first. I was reluctant, but now I'm glad I've come."

"Just be careful of *Mamm*—she'll try to matchmake you," Martha said with a giggle. "She just can't help yourself."

"Hush, Martha," Esther reprimanded her.

Martha pulled a face. "Why, you know it's true!"

Hannah rubbed her eyes. It certainly was true. She sincerely hoped if her mother had indeed given up trying to marry her to David Yoder that she wouldn't try to foist him on the unsuspecting Mary.

"Are you interested in any boys back home?" Martha asked her.

"Martha!" Esther said. "I don't know what's come over you tonight."

Hannah lightly touched Mary's arm. "Just ignore my two younger *schweschders*. They have boys on their minds."

"We do not," Esther said, "and why do you blame your younger *schweschders*? I haven't said a word, have I? It was Martha who said it, not me. Every time Martha does something wrong, you always say it's your younger *schweschders*, but it's never me, it's Martha. It's always Martha."

"No, it isn't," Martha said. "I'm sure you said something too. Didn't she say something too, Mary?"

Mary and Hannah exchanged glances. "Anyway, you didn't tell us if you're interested in any boys," Martha persisted, ignoring a warning glance from Hannah.

"No, the boys in my community aren't interested in me," Mary said sadly.

"Why ever not?" Martha asked her.

"It's like my *bruder* said—the people in our community only like thin, attractive people. I rather like my food too much, I'm afraid." She patted her stomach.

"I'm sure that's not true," Hannah said by way of consolation. "Who looks at the outward appearance?"

She meant it as a rhetorical question, but Mary answered. "All the boys in my community, I'm afraid."

Mrs. Miller cleared her throat and abruptly stood up. "Hannah, come and help me in the kitchen."

Mary made to stand up too, but Mrs. Miller waved her down. "Mary, you can help from tomorrow, but not tonight. Tonight you are our guest, so please relax and have dinner with us."

Mary looked happy.

As soon as they reached the kitchen, Mrs. Miller indicated that Hannah should get the potatoes out of the oven.

"But, *Mamm*, I can't, not on my crutches," Hannah protested.

Mrs. Miller rubbed her chin. "How silly of me. I keep forgetting. All right then, I'll pull a chair over to the stove for you. You can sit down and make the gravy. *Sell kann ennichpepper duh.*" *Anyone can do that.*

Hannah set about melting the butter in the pan her mother had set in front of her, but it wasn't long before her mother spoke again. "So what do you think of John?" she asked Hannah.

"They both seem very nice," Hannah said, with emphasis on the word *both.*

Her mother was not so easily distracted. "Yes, they're both nice, but I wanted to know what you thought of John in particular. He seems a fine man, doesn't he?"

"Yes." Hannah turned her attention back to the gravy. She drizzled in the chicken stock and whisked.

Mrs. Miller banged a pot down, and Hannah looked up, startled. Obviously she had done something to make her mother angry.

"Hannah, you act as if I'm against you, but I'm only trying to help you. You're twenty-one now, and that's past the marrying age. Why, in some communities you'd be considered an old maid! The time is running out for you to find a suitable *mann* and have *kinner.* Why, before you know it, you'll be too old to have *kinner.* The years pass by in a flash, I'm telling you." She put her hands on her hips.

"But, but," Hannah sputtered.

Her mother held up one hand, palm outward. "Hannah, I only have your best interests at heart. Do you wish to stay with your *vadder* and me, in this *haus*, forever?" Without waiting for Hannah to answer, she pushed on. "Of course not. Every woman should find herself a good husband."

Hannah finally dared to speak. "Shouldn't a husband find me?"

Her mother made a strangled sound at the back of her throat. "Well, that's precisely what they're trying to do, Hannah," she said in a stern tone. "David Yoder has shown you his attentions, but you've refused them, and now John's as well. Where will it all end?" She threw both her hands in the air.

"John hasn't shown me any attentions at all," Hannah said, puzzled.

Mrs. Miller banged another pot. "Give him time, Hannah. He's not betrothed, and he doesn't have his eye on another girl. Why wouldn't he be interested in you? Besides, he said the girls in his community don't find him attractive for some reason. That means he will be more inclined to be interested in you."

Hannah tried to process what her mother had just said. "Are you saying he's desperate to find a *fraa* so he'll take anyone?"

Mrs. Miller slammed another pot down, harder than before. "This is not an amusing situation, Hannah. Before you know it, you'll be old and alone and living in the *grossmammi haus* of one of your *schweschders*. Is that what you want?"

"No," Hannah began, but her mother silenced her.

"You need to find a man, and now you have two to choose from—David Yoder and John Beiler."

"But I don't even know if John likes me," Hannah protested.

Her mother shook her head furiously. "Honestly, I don't know what's wrong with you, Hannah. He's only just met you. Be nice to him."

"But I don't like him," Hannah said, whisking the gravy even more furiously. She was worried her mother was speaking so loudly that the others might overhear.

"No woman likes a man on first meeting," Mrs. Miller said. "Attraction grows slowly. Besides, *Gott* has appointed a man for every woman and a woman for every man. You should not resist the one *Gott* has put in your path."

Hannah sighed and did her best not to roll her eyes. Her mother no doubt thought *Gott* had put David Yoder or John Beiler in her path. The only man she had ever wanted was Noah Hostetler, and look how that had turned out!

Maybe she would be better off being alone and living in the *grossmammi haus* of one of her *schweschders* in her old age, after all, if the only alternatives were David Yoder and John Beiler. Not that she had any objection to John—he seemed nice. In fact, she thought he would make a good friend, but as for a husband? She sincerely doubted that. He didn't make her heart flutter like Noah had right from the moment she had first laid eyes on him.

Her mother's words brought her back to reality. "Hannah, help me with this food."

Hannah hurried out of the kitchen, pleased to be away from her *mudder's* lecturing. She knew her *mudder* did only have her best interests at heart, but there was no way Hannah intended to be married to a man she didn't love.

Chapter Six

When Hannah opened her eyes after the silent prayer, she thought John was looking straight at her. She offered him a small smile, but he looked away at once. *Oh dear, I hope he isn't attracted to me*, Hannah thought. *Or maybe he's just shy.*

She had thought her mother was overly keen to marry her to David Yoder, but after the conversation they'd just had in the kitchen, it was clear her mother was keen to marry her to the first man who came along. It dawned on her that her mother just wanted her married, and whoever the husband was not so much of a concern. "Oh great," she said aloud.

All eyes on the table turned to her.

"What did you say?" Esther said.

"I'm just thinking aloud," she said, and shoveled some chicken into her mouth, so no one could ask her anything else.

"We'll have the *grossmammi haus* ready for you in no time," Mr. Miller said to Mary.

"Denki," she said. "Please don't go to any trouble on my account."

"It will be our pleasure," Mr. Miller said. "It's already furnished, of course. It just hasn't been used in a while, so Mrs. Miller and Hannah will give it a good clean tomorrow."

Mary nodded. "Please allow me to help you. After all, the bishop did send me here to help you."

Mr. Miller made to protest, but Mrs. Miller spoke up. "I think that's a *gut* idea, Mary. *Denki.* That way, we'll have it finished tomorrow and then perhaps you could move here tomorrow afternoon, that is, if John doesn't mind bringing you back?"

John muttered something through a mouthful of potatoes.

Mrs. Miller leaned across the table. "I'm sorry. I didn't catch what you said."

He swallowed hurriedly and then coughed hard. Mrs. Miller stood up and patted him hard on his back.

"Now, now, Rachel, leave the poor boy alone," Mr. Miller said.

Mrs. Miller shook her head. "Can't you see he's choking, Abraham! Here, John, drink this water."

John took a gulp of water. Hannah felt sorry for him because he did appear awfully embarrassed. "Sorry about that. I said I'd be happy to bring Mary back tomorrow."

Mrs. Miller gave him a nod of approval. "Now John, if you're recovered, please tell us about your life in your community."

John's face went beet red, no doubt as he did not like to be the center of attention. "Well, it's just like anyone else's life, I suppose," he said doubtfully. "I get up; I drink a lot of *kaffi*; I do farm work; I come in for lunch; I do more farming; I eat a lot and then I go to sleep."

Mrs. Miller nodded encouragingly. "*Gut*, so you're a hard worker then. No doubt a *fraa* would be a big help to you. So do you do all your own cooking?"

John gave a rueful smile. "I'm afraid so."

"Well then, you need a *fraa* to help you, don't you?"

John's face went an even deeper shade of red, and he muttered something.

Hannah was relieved when Mr. Miller spoke. "That was a hearty meal," he said. "And what's next, Rachel? Shoo Fly Pie? Graham Cracker Pudding? Apple Dumplings?"

"Layered pudding, vanilla cornstarch pudding, and banana pudding," she said. "We just have to wait for Hannah and Martha to finish eating. They are always the slowest."

"How can I be any faster since I have to eat with my left hand?" Martha stopped speaking as soon as her mother shot her a withering glare.

"What's your excuse, Hannah?" Mrs. Miller said, but then must have thought she shouldn't harangue Hannah in front of John, so quickly added, "Hannah is a big help to me, especially with her *schweschders* injured. The doctor said Hannah had to rest up, but she can't. That's where you'll be a big help, Mary."

"Yes, I'm happy to help," Mary said. Hannah noticed that Mary was a lot more outgoing and talkative than her *bruder.* "It must have been terrible, all of you in that buggy accident."

"Hush, Mary," John said in muted tones. "The bishop said you're not to mention the accident."

Mary clamped her hand over her mouth. "I'm so sorry. Me and my big mouth. My *mudder* says every time I open my mouth, I put my foot in it."

"Don't worry about it at all," Mrs. Miller said. "We live with the consequences of that accident every day so it's hardly something we've forgotten. Please don't feel bad."

Mr. Miller cleared his throat. "Hannah won't be much help to you, Rachel, with cleaning the *grossmammi haus* tomorrow. Now that Mary is helping you, I'm certain the two of you will be able to manage it together."

Mrs. Miller narrowed her eyes. "I'm not sure what you mean."

"The *doktor* said Hannah should rest up, and being on crutches, I don't think she would be much help to you. I'm sure you and Mary can manage together."

Mrs. Miller bit her lip. Finally, she said, "Aha! You want Hannah to start at Katie Hostetler's shop tomorrow, don't you!" Without waiting for him to answer, she pushed on. "That's work, isn't it? Why can Hannah work in that quilt store, if she can't work here?"

Mr. Miller did not look in the least perturbed. "Because the work she will be doing there no doubt will be sitting down and sewing rather than cleaning and doing physical work," he explained patiently.

Mrs. Miller's cheeks flushed red. First, two red spots appeared on each cheek, and the spots grew bigger and bigger. "I don't think it's a good idea at all," Mrs. Miller through gritted teeth.

Hannah knew her mother did not want her working for Katie Hostetler. In fact, her mother would be happy if none of them ever saw a Hostetler again.

"Hostetler," Mary said. "Wasn't it a Hostetler who caused your buggy accident?"

John's face turned white. "Mary!" he admonished her.

"Yes, it was a Hostetler," Mrs. Miller said.

"And of course we have to forgive," Mr. Miller said, casting a sideways glance at his wife. "And Hannah will soon start working for Mrs. Hostetler."

It was obvious to Hannah that Mary wanted to know more, and Hannah figured she was having trouble remaining silent. Mrs. Miller left the table and in a short time could be heard banging pots and pans around in the kitchen.

Mr. Hostetler wiped one hand across his brow. "John, would you please help me bring in some more firewood?"

John and Mr. Miller left while Mary turned to the

girls. "I'm so sorry. I told you I had a big mouth. I think I've upset your mother."

"No, you haven't," Hannah said.

"I don't think *Mamm* has forgiven the Hostetlers," Martha said.

"Martha!" Hannah and Esther said in unison.

"Well, she hasn't," Martha said. "Why else would she be so upset about you going to work for Mrs. Hostetler, Hannah? She doesn't have anything to do with the Hostetlers now, not after what happened. I mean, even before it happened *Mamm* always said Mrs. Hostetler wasn't strict enough for her liking."

"Martha!" Hannah said again.

Martha ignored her and pushed on. "You know how she always says Mrs. Hostetler's glasses look gold? *Mamm* says Mrs. Hostetler might as well wear jewelry as wear those glasses. She's always complaining and saying that Mrs. Hostetler should wear wire-rimmed glasses."

Things were going from bad to worse. Hannah desperately tried to think of something so she could change the subject.

"I heard it was one of the sons who was driving," Mary finally ventured to ask.

"Jah," Martha said. "There are four Hostetler brothers, and we're good friends with them all—or we were. Noah was driving."

"That must be awkward, seeing you're all in the same community," Mary said. "How old is Noah?"

"He's Hannah's age." Martha avoided looking at

Hannah. "Hannah was sweet on him before the accident."

Hannah kicked Martha under the table.

"Ouch!" Martha shrieked. "Why did you do that, Hannah? I'm sure I have a bruise." She leaned under the table to rub her leg.

Mary's eyes darted around the room wildly. Hannah wondered if people in Mary's community were so unruly. Perhaps this behavior was a shock to her.

Just then, Mr. Miller and John returned to the house each with an armful of wood. They placed it in the wood basket near the fire. Mr. Miller stoked the fire and indicated that John should sit back down.

Mrs. Miller entered the room with a large pot of what Hannah assumed was meadow tea, but her face was as black as a thundercloud.

An uncomfortable silence descended over the table. "So, is it settled then?" Mrs. Miller asked her husband. "Hannah will start working for Katie Hostetler tomorrow?"

Mr. Miller stroked his graying beard. *"Jah,"* he said firmly.

Hannah rubbed her temples. She was sure a headache was brewing. Things were going rapidly downhill. Now her mother had found two suitors for her, and she was to work for Noah Hostetler's mother. Could it get any worse?

Yes, it could, if Noah showed up at the store. Surely he wouldn't be so silly. Surely his mother would order him to keep away. But what if he did?

What would she do? She had not spoken to him since that fateful day.

That night, Hannah had barely any sleep. Finally, she got off the mattress and opened the curtains so she could return to the mattress and watch the moon and the stars behind the large hickory trees. The one good thing was that Mary would take some of the burden, and then Hannah knew her leg would heal faster for getting the rest. And while John was pleasant enough, she hoped he would go back to his community sooner rather than later, and then she would only have David Yoder to content with.

Sleep continued to elude her, so she walked into the kitchen to make some chamomile tea.

As soon as she sat at the kitchen table with her tea, Esther came into the room. "I didn't wake you, I hope?" Hannah said. "Did me walking in here wake you or did the moonlight wake you when I opened the curtains? I wouldn't have done it if I thought you would wake up."

"*Nee*, you didn't wake me. I wake a few times in the night because my back hurts and I have to readjust my sleeping position. Why are you awake, Hannah? You usually snore all through the night."

"I don't snore!" Hannah said with horror. "Do I?"

Esther laughed. "Yes, you do. But in a cute way, not like a pig."

"Well, that's good—I suppose," Hannah said, rolling her eyes. "Mary's going to be a big help, isn't she?"

Esther winked at her. "What did you think of John?"

Hannah groaned. "Not you too! You're as bad as *Mamm*."

Esther laughed. "I'm only teasing. I know you're in love with Noah." As soon as she said the words, she gasped and slammed her hand over her mouth. "I'm sorry. I didn't mean to say it."

A knot formed in the pit of Hannah's stomach. "*Nee*, that's all right. I was, before…well, you know. That's why I can't sleep now. I'm worried that I'll see him at his mother's quilt store."

"I'm sure you won't," Esther said. "His mother would tell him you're working for her and warn him to stay away."

"I do hope you're right," Hannah said. Yet an often-suppressed part of her secretly hoped she would see Noah Hostetler, and that, in fact, was the very thing that kept her awake.

Chapter Seven

Hannah hobbled up the road on her crutches, making her way to Mrs. Hostetler's quilt store. She knew where it was, but had never taken much notice of it. Now, she stood in front of it, taking in the gloomy appearance of the discolored, dark wood planks.

Hannah's mood matched the building's exterior. She was tired and had been unable to follow the doctor's instructions to keep off her leg, as much as she had dearly wanted to. The only rest she ever got was at night, on the mattress, which was not exactly what the doctor had in mind. Her arms ached from the crutches and she had developed a sore back. Her supporting leg ached most of the time.

Still, her three sisters were worse off. There was nothing else for it—Hannah needed to visit Rebecca in the hospital, and help her already overworked *mudder* care for Esther and Martha. At least, sewing for Mrs. Hostetler was something she could do while sitting down. That was something for which she was grateful.

Hannah knew Mrs. Hostetler from the church meeting every second Sunday and of course, they were both in the same community. However, since the accident, the Hostetlers and her *familye* had been doing their best to avoid each other. Hannah knew this was her *mudder's* doing.

Hannah poked her head around the door, and looked straight into the face of Mrs. Hostetler who was hovering just inside. Hannah barely had time to look around the store's interior before Mrs. Hostetler took her by the arm and guided her to a room at the back of the store.

"Sit, sit. Take some weight off your leg. I'll make us each a nice cup of hot mint tea." Her voice was kindly.

Mrs. Hostetler went off to make the tea and Hannah stared at the obvious signs of electricity, not the least of which was the electric heater facing her.

Mrs. Hostetler returned and smiled. "I rent this place," she said, nodding at the electric heater.

Hannah wondered what that meant and made a mental note to ask someone. She knew electricity was permitted outside the home in most cases, and her *daed's* store had electricity, but she didn't know that smaller stores were permitted to use it. Hannah shrugged. She really had no idea about such matters, and figured Mrs. Hostetler could hardly install a wood fire in a small rented store.

Mrs. Hostetler set a steaming hot mug of mint tea in

front of Hannah, as well as a large piece of *Melassich Riwwelkuche*, Shoo-Fly Pie. "Eat," she encouraged. "It will warm you up, to have something inside you." She patted her own tummy.

Hannah at once relaxed. *Mrs. Hostetler is very friendly. I always remember her as being very nice*, she thought. *She must be awfully embarrassed that her son caused the accident.*

While Hannah ate, Mrs. Hostetler asked after her sisters. Hannah tried to gloss over their injuries due to a sense of compassion toward Mrs. Hostetler. After all, Mrs. Hostetler wasn't the one who had driven into their buggy and caused the accident.

"And now I'll tell you about your duties here," Mrs. Hostetler continued, "but please call me Katie."

Hannah nodded, a little embarrassed.

"Now, down to business. This store sells mainly quilts, but also wall hangings and quillows—you know, a quilt and pillow combined."

Hannah continued to nod.

"Everything is hand done, but I use a sewing machine to piece the quilts. It would take far too long otherwise, and I'm already getting behind with orders." Katie nodded to the door to the main section of the store. "I have a foot-operated, treadle sewing machine out there. The *Englisch* customers are intrigued by it." Katie laughed, but then looked somber. "I won't get you to sew on it yet, not with your leg."

Hannah made to protest. "It's my left leg that's injured, and I'm sure I could use my right leg on the treadle. I'm sure I could manage."

Katie looked doubtful. "But surely, before—" she broke off and caught her breath "—the accident, you used both feet?"

"Yes, Mrs. Hostetler, um, sorry, Katie, but I'm sure it would be easy enough to do with one foot. I don't think the cast would get in the way. I'm certain I could figure it out." Hannah was worried that Katie Hostetler hadn't taken her leg into consideration when she had wanted to employ her and had been hoping she would sew on the machine.

Katie Hostetler cleared the plates and cups away. "When your leg is out of its cast, of course you may piece the quilts, but I have plenty of sewing for you to do before that."

Hannah breathed a sigh of relief.

"I sew in the front of the store," Katie Hostetler continued, "as the *Englischers* like to see me sewing, and it's easier to serve customers if I'm already out there. There's plenty of room for us both to sit out there, and we can chat as we sew."

Hannah's heart fell. As nice as Katie Hostetler was, Hannah did not wish to spend hours chatting to her. What could they have to talk about? Hannah's sisters, injured by Katie Hostetler's son? Hannah's mother, who was just as upset with Katie Hostetler's son, Noah, as Hannah herself was?

This is going to be awkward, Hannah thought. She hoped that Katie Hostetler had plenty of work to do on the treadle, which would make talking over the noise difficult.

By lunchtime, Hannah's fears had abated. She

was more relaxed and even enjoying herself. Katie Hostetler had talked about aspects of quilting all morning, much to Hannah's delight. Hannah had always been keen on sewing.

"Lunch time," Katie suddenly announced.

Hannah was embarrassed. She hadn't thought to bring lunch with her, as she wasn't sure how long she would be working that first day.

Katie gasped. "Hannah, I'm so thoughtless. I should've said that I wanted you to work until three today, but only to midday other days. Never mind, I have plenty of lunch here for you."

Hannah made to protest, but then stopped herself. "*Denki*, Mrs. Hostetler."

"Remember I said to call me Katie." With that, Katie smiled and went into the back room. After a minute or two, she poked her head around the door. "Come on, Hannah, lunch."

Hannah stood up, and immediately noticed that her back pain had gone and her arms weren't aching. *The morning's rest, sitting down, has done me a power of good*, she thought.

Hannah hadn't realized how hungry she was until she saw the little table laden with *schnitz und knepp*, ham and apple dumplings. As she sat down on the wooden chair, she looked around for a cookstove but couldn't see one.

Katie laughed. "I use a small gas cookstove, just over there. Anyway, how did you find the morning's work?"

Hannah smiled. "I enjoyed it, *denki*."

"Your sewing is very good. Do you make quilts?"

Hannah looked up, surprised, and then realized that Katie was asking her if she made quilts at home, not quilts in her shop. "*Jah*, I do."

Katie set a plate of *schnitz und knepp* in front of Hannah. "If you're interested, I could sell your quilts here on commission. They do bring good prices here."

"*Jah*, I saw." Hannah had been surprised at the high prices of quilts in Katie Hostetler's store. This could be a further way to help her parents' financial problems over the medical expenses.

The bell over the door sounded and Katie Hostetler went into the front room to attend to the customer. Hannah followed, but far more slowly. As she opened the door she heard Mrs. Hostetler hiss words such as *"Ferhoodled,"* confused, mixed up, and *"Ab im kopp,"* crazy. Surely Mrs. Hostetler wouldn't be speaking to a customer like that?

Hannah hesitated, wondering if she should enter the room, but she was there to work after all. No doubt Mrs. Hostetler would take the person into the back room if she wanted to have a private conversation with him or her.

Hannah hobbled forward on her crutches, only to look up into the face of Noah Hostetler.

"You!"

Hannah's word came out as an accusation, but she had no time to mind that, as in surprise, she stepped forward without her crutches and fell forward hard onto the floor.

It seemed to happen in slow motion and she saw both Mrs. Hostetler and Noah start toward her, shock on their faces.

Noah reached her first, and helped her to her feet.

"Denki." Hannah knew the word had come out stiffly, but she was fortunate that she had managed to speak at all. Noah's proximity had set her heart racing, and vibrations were running through her at his touch. She felt as though she had placed her hand on a generator. Her breath came in short bursts.

Mrs. Hostler reached her and helped her to a chair, her face full of concern.

"I'm fine; I'm fine," Hannah protested to Mrs. Hostetler, who was bending over her while at the same time nodding to the door in an obvious attempt to get Noah to leave. "I'm just *doplich*."

"You're not clumsy, Hannah." Mrs. Hostetler fussed over her like a mother hen. "Are you hurt?"

"Nee." Only my heart is hurt, Hannah thought. She looked past Mrs. Hostetler, but Noah had gone. He had left the store.

Why did her heart race so when she saw him?

How could her feelings for him still be there after everything Noah Hostetler had done to her, and not only to her, but to her sisters too?

Noah stumbled out the door, heartbroken. This was the first time he had spoken to Hannah since the accident. The very first word she had said to him had been nothing less than an accusation.

She must really hate me, he thought despondently.

And who can blame her? If it weren't for me, Hannah and her three schweschders *wouldn't be injured. It's all my fault. I'm sure she'll hate me forever.*

The bishop had warned Noah to keep away from Hannah's *mudder*, Mrs. Miller, as it would likely take her some time to come to terms with the accident. Even the kindly Mr. Miller had told Noah the same thing. Noah was surprised that Hannah had agreed to work for his own *mudder*, but he figured that Mr. Miller must have had a hand it, perhaps to try to force reconciliation between the *familyes*.

It had been a mistake to come here today; Noah knew that now. Yet it was so hard for him to keep away from Hannah. Right before the accident, he had been about to tell her his feelings for her. Now his hopes and dreams had all been cruelly shattered, just because he'd gotten behind the wheel of the car that day. The worst thing of all was he had no one to blame but himself.

Chapter Eight

Hannah stood with hesitation at the front doors of the hospital, as she did every time. She stood there silently talking herself into entering. As always, it was a war within her.

Finally, she took a deep breath and stepped inside. As she walked down the hospital corridors as she had done countless times before, she focused on Rebecca. Rebecca would be awfully disappointed if she didn't visit with her, but that fact did not help the reluctance that always overcame her. Every time she saw a doctor, the sight filled her with dread. She knew doctors helped people, but the therapist had explained to her that fears are sometimes irrational.

She wished she could turn tail and run, but not only would Rebecca be upset, but she was unable to run on her crutches.

Hannah forced herself on, one foot after the other. At least hospitals no longer had the overpowering antiseptic odor they'd had when she visited her *gross-*

dawdi in hospital many years earlier, when she was a child. These days, hospitals seemed far less clinical—at least, this one was.

Hannah continued on, telling herself cheerful facts about the hospital. When she reached Rebecca's room, she walked right on through.

Rebecca quickly shoved something under her pillow.

"What are you hiding from me?" Hannah asked her.

Rebecca exhaled long and hard. "Oh, it's you, Hannah! What a relief. I thought it was one of the nurses." She pulled out a little amber bottle and showed it to Hannah. "It's just my arnica tincture. Mrs. Graber gave it to me, but one of the nurses doesn't like me having it. She tried to take it away from me."

Hannah was puzzled. "Did Mrs. Graber only just give this to you now? She gave me arnica tincture weeks ago."

Rebecca shook her head. "*Nee*. She gave it to me after the accident, and she keeps bringing me more when I run out. The other nurses haven't minded. It's just a new nurse I've never met. She doesn't seem all that friendly either."

"Oh." Hannah walked to look out the window. One side of the hospital overlooked a large park, and Hannah idly watched the children playing far below.

"Hannah, are you listening to me?"

Hannah spun around. "Yes. Oh, I mean no, probably not," she amended. "Sorry, what did you say?"

Rebecca bit her lip. "You're distracted today, Hannah." When Hannah did not respond, she continued. "So, sit here. Tell me all about Mary and John." She patted the edge of her bed.

Hannah walked a couple of steps and sat on the edge of Rebecca's bed. "They seem very nice."

"Nice?" Rebecca shrieked. "Nice? I want to know all about them and you just give me a one-word answer?"

Hannah shrugged. "Well, I don't know what else to say. They do seem very nice. Mary is going to fit in well with our family."

Rebecca giggled. "Mary obviously isn't married, so *Mamm's* going to try to play the matchmaker, isn't she?"

Hannah laughed. "Most likely, but who with? I hope not with David Yoder."

"*Nee!* Don't tell me you want him for yourself."

Hannah gasped in horror. "Of course not! No! I don't mean to say unkind things, but I think there's something about him that's somewhat untrustworthy and I wouldn't like to see Mary with him."

Rebecca nodded slowly. "Oh yes, I see what you mean. Now tell me about John. What is John like?"

"He seems nice too," Hannah said.

"Nice!" Rebecca said. "Don't tell me this nice business. Tell me more about him. Is he married?"

"*Nee*, and he's not betrothed either," Hannah said automatically.

Rebecca raised her eyebrows. "So, are you interested in him?"

Hannah shook her head. "He seems nice enough, but I don't feel any spark."

Rebecca shot her a speculative look. "Like you feel with Noah."

"Like I *felt* with Noah," Hannah corrected her.

A nurse bustled in. "I'm sorry, Rebecca. We need this extra chair," she said. Another nurse appeared and the two of them wrestled a large reclining chair out of Rebecca's room.

"The second nurse who came in is the one who complained about Mrs. Graber's arnica tincture," Rebecca said. "The first nurse is nice."

Hannah nodded and resisted the urge to tease Rebecca for calling someone nice. "Yes, I recognized the first nurse. I've seen her a lot."

"Anyway, I have *gut* news. My regular hospital physical therapist is pleased with my improvement."

A wave of relief hit Hannah. "*Wunderbar!* No wonder you seem in high spirits."

"I am, but let's talk about you. Noah is still in love with you, Hannah."

Hannah gasped. "Hush, Rebecca. You mustn't say such a thing."

Rebecca folded her arms. "Why not? It's the truth."

Hannah shook her head. "How do you know it's the truth?" Without waiting for her sister to answer, she pushed on. "Besides, it doesn't matter how Noah feels. It only matters how I feel."

"And how do you feel?" Rebecca asked her.

"I haven't come here to speak about Noah

Hostetler," Hannah said in a firm voice. "I've come here to see you. How are you feeling? Is the arnica tincture helping you?"

Thankfully, her attempt to change the subject appeared to be successful. "*Jah*, I'm sure it has helped. The nurses said they were surprised the bruises subsided so quickly."

"That's good," Hannah said. "I'm sure *Mamm* will bring Mary to visit you one day soon, so you'll be able to meet her." She was saying anything she could to stop the subject falling back to Noah Hostetler.

"So what does she look like?" Rebecca asked her. "Is she old? Is she young? *Mamm* said she was young, but she didn't tell me her age."

"I suppose she's about my age, twenty-one," Hannah said.

Rebecca giggled again. "Oh, that will upset *Mamm*! Twenty-one and not married. You watch—*Mamm* will have her married soon."

Hannah joined in the laughter.

"And is she tall? And is she thin? *Mamm* will try to fatten her up."

"No, she is neither tall nor thin," Hannah said. "She has brown eyes and brown hair. Anyway, I'm sure you'll meet her for yourself soon enough."

"I won't meet John, will I?" Rebecca said. "*Mamm* told me he was only here for a few days to bring his *schweschder*?"

Hannah shrugged one shoulder. "John is not thin, and he's not tall. I suppose he's about my height. He has brown hair and brown eyes too," she said, as she knew that would be the next question her sister would ask her.

"Does he have a sense of humor?" Rebecca pressed her.

Hannah nodded. "*Jah*, and he does seem awfully nice." She laughed as she said the word *nice* once more.

Rebecca scrunched up her face. "Hannah, it's getting a little cold. Would you please put that blanket over my legs?"

Hannah slowly lowered herself from the bed. She fetched a white blanket from the remaining spare chair over by the window. She idly wondered why hospital blankets were white. The hospital would have to do a lot of laundry, and every spot would show on the white blankets and white sheets.

Hannah yawned and stretched as soon as she laid out the blanket.

"Are you all right, Hannah? You look more tired than usual."

Hannah shook her head and sat back down on the bed. "Actually, I feel more rested than I have been in a long time. It's going to help that Mary's here, but working in Mrs. Hostetler's store lets me sit down for hours at a time and that helps, too."

Rebecca let out a shriek and then clamped her hand over her mouth. "What! Why didn't you tell me you are working for Mrs. Hostetler? Why did you want to keep it a secret from me?"

Hannah hurried to placate Rebecca. "*Nee*, I wasn't keeping it a secret from you. *Datt* only just told me I should work for Mrs. Hostetler. Today was my first day. I wasn't keeping it from you, truly."

Rebecca appeared only somewhat mollified. "Truly?"

Hannah nodded. "Of course. I forgot you didn't know."

Some color returned to Rebecca's cheeks. "Go on then. Tell me all about it."

Hannah shrugged. "There's nothing to tell. *Datt* wanted me to work for Mrs. Hostetler, that's all. My first day was today."

Rebecca's eyebrows shot skyward. "I'll bet *Mamm* wasn't happy about that."

"No, she wasn't," Hannah admitted. "I'm sure she'll come around in time."

Rebecca remained silent.

"I actually enjoy working there," Hannah said. "Like I said, I sit down and don't have to speak with customers. It gives my leg a rest."

"But what if Noah comes in?" Rebecca asked her. "Would you actually speak with him? What would you do?" When Hannah didn't answer, Rebecca let out another shriek. "He did come in, didn't he! Don't try to deny it, because you've gone as white as a sheet that's been hanging out in the sun for days."

Hannah rubbed her forehead furiously with one hand. "He came into the store and then left abruptly when he saw me," she told her younger sister.

"There's more to it, isn't there?" Rebecca narrowed her eyes.

"No, that was all."

Hannah hobbled over to the window and stared down at the park below.

Was Rebecca right? Was Noah still in love with her? And if he was, why would that matter to her?

When Hannah arrived home that night, she was happier than she had been in quite some time.

Further, Hannah had enjoyed chatting with Katie Hostetler, but even more, had enjoyed the good rest that the hours of sitting had afforded her. In fact, the only parts of her that hurt somewhat were her eyes, from long periods of close stitching. Her leg did not pain her for the first time since the accident. Perhaps with Mary helping her *mudder*, Hannah's leg would be able to heal, after all.

Of course, seeing Noah was a shock, and she knew she should be upset about that. Still, for some reason she was in high spirits.

Hannah's heart was singing but that did not last when she entered the *haus* and saw their dinner guest was David Yoder. She silently berated herself for being surprised. Her *mudder* had been doing her best to be a matchmaker and had her heart set on Hannah marrying David. Before the accident, her *mudder* had approved of Hannah's attraction to Noah Hostetler, but of course that had all changed.

David's face lighted up when he saw Hannah and she did her best to smile. She was not attracted to David, not in the slightest. He was good-looking enough, being tall and wiry, but he always had an arrogant manner about him and a cold, thin-lipped smile on his face. There was no warmth about him whatsoever. She had even heard rumors that he had been seen with *Englisch* girls.

David continued to stare at Hannah. *He's looking me over like I'm a cow at the market*, Hannah thought, and she could not suppress an involuntary shudder.

On the other hand, Mrs. Miller clearly did not share her opinion of David. She gushed all over him. "Look who's here, Hannah."

Hannah resisted the urge to say something sarcastic, and merely said, "*Hiya*, David."

"*Hiya*, Hannah." His voice dripped honey, and he winked at Hannah.

"Have you met Mary?"

Mrs. Miller snorted. "Of course he's met Mary, Hannah. Have you taken leave of your senses? Mary is sitting right there. Do you think I would neglect to introduce David to Mary?"

Hannah wondered what she had done to upset her *mudder*. "Has John returned home?" Hannah asked, hoping she could divert the attention from herself.

It was Mary who answered. "*Nee*, he's having dinner with the Fischers. I've officially moved in here now."

Hannah's face lit up. "That's *wunderbar*! So you and *Mamm* finished preparing the *grossmammi haus* today?"

Mary nodded. "*Jah*. John brought my belongings over today. He'll be going home in a few days."

"Who is John?" David asked. There was an edge to his tone.

"John is Mary's *bruder*," Hannah said, irritated at the obvious note of jealousy in David's voice.

David looked most displeased. "Did his *fraa* accompany him here?"

"He doesn't have a *fraa*, and he's not betrothed," Hannah said, somewhat guilty that she had said that to upset David, even though he had no right to be upset.

Mrs. Miller's hand flew to her mouth. "Oh, silly me. I forgot to collect the eggs. Hannah, would you and David go collect the eggs for me?"

David leaped to his feet, but Hannah stood there staring at her mother. "But, *Mamm*, it's night, and besides, the chickens aren't laying at this time of year."

Her *mudder's* face turned beet red, and Hannah at once realized that this was a matchmaking ploy. "Okay, *Mamm*," she said, before her mother could rebuke her. The last thing she wanted was any time alone with David, but her *mudder* had other ideas.

Hannah put on her warm mittens and her long wool coat. She considered asking Mary if she would accompany her, but knew that would only serve to make her *mudder* even angrier.

Hannah hobbled out to the barn. David hurried after her, holding the lantern aloft. She figured that if she kept ahead of him, there would be less opportunity to speak with him. As soon as Hannah reached the coop, she walked inside and shut the door behind her. She hurried to look in the nest boxes despite knowing that there were no eggs, but then she could at least say she had looked. She turned around and hurried out of the coop as best she could on her crutches.

When the latch was shut, Hannah turned back toward the *haus*, but David was standing directly in front of her. She was unable to step back, so quickly took a step to the side. David attempted to put his arm around her waist, but she pulled away.

"David Yoder!" Hannah said by way of rebuke.

David removed his arm, but blocked her way. "Hannah, I was wondering if you'd come on a buggy ride with me one afternoon."

"*Nee*, David," she snapped, and made to push past him. Hannah felt bad for snapping, but she most certainly did not want to date David Yoder. She had heard rumors that he'd been seen with *Englisch* girls and at the time had paid the rumors no mind, but his act of trying to put his arm around her in a darkened barn did not improve her opinion of him. That was most certainly inappropriate behavior. She had never given him any encouragement whatsoever. Still, she wished that she had turned down his invitation graciously, but his physical proximity had alarmed her.

"I'm afraid of buggies, after the accident," she added in a more measured tone.

David reached for her hand but she pulled it away. "Is that why you won't come on a buggy ride with me, as you're scared of buggies now." He said it more as a statement than a question.

"Nee." Hannah wished she hadn't opened her big mouth and made that remark about buggies, as she could see why it had given David the wrong idea.

Still, David was persistent. "Are you seeing anyone else?"

"Nee," Hannah said again, before thinking. It was none of David's business whether or not she was seeing anyone.

"Is it Noah Hostetler? You always were following him around. I thought him causing your accident would cure you of him. Or is it John?"

David loomed over her, so close that she could feel his breath on her cheek. Hannah pushed him away, hard, and then hurried back to the *haus* as fast as she could.

When Hannah reached the *haus*, her sisters were already sitting at the table. Esther shot her a worried look. Hannah headed for the kitchen but her mother waved her back. "Mary will help me serve."

Mary and Mrs. Miller served *Dutch Goose* to the *familye*. Dutch Goose took a lot of preparation, so Hannah knew that David was an expected dinner guest—he hadn't just turned up. It had to be baked for around three hours. Hannah suspected Mrs. Miller would not have made Dutch Goose had Mary been the only expected guest. If only her mother would abandon her matchmaking plans! Hannah did want to marry, but she wanted to marry a man who made her heart race.

After the silent prayer, Hannah stole a look at David. He seemed to be in a sulky mood. He had certainly gone quiet.

"How was Rebecca today, Hannah?" Mr. Miller asked Hannah.

Hannah put down her fork. "Oh, she was doing well. She was happy because her physical therapist is pleased with her progress. I'm sorry I didn't tell you—I don't know how I forgot it."

Mrs. Miller made a point of winking at her and then nodded at David. "That's all right. I know you had other things on your mind."

Esther rolled her eyes and Hannah rubbed her temples. She wondered if she could pretend she was getting a headache and excuse herself, although the mattresses were nearby so she could hardly escape upstairs. No, there was nothing for it—she was stuck here for a long, painful night evening with David Yoder.

Hannah caught Mary looking speculatively between her and David. "Are you two friends?" Mary asked.

"Yes," David said, before Hannah had a chance to speak.

Hannah wondered what she could say that was tactful. She couldn't come up with anything, so she remained silent.

Thankfully, Mr. Miller came to her rescue. "David is the son of my wife's best friend, Beth, therefore he has known all my *dochders* for years and so is friends with all of them."

Mary nodded, although Hannah thought she looked puzzled.

After everyone had finished the Dutch Goose, Hannah stood up, but once more her mother told her to sit down. "Mary can help me clear the table," she said. "You sit there and speak with David."

Hannah squirmed in her seat. David did try to engage her in conversation, but she only gave him one-word answers so he eventually gave up. It wasn't long before Mrs. Miller and Mary returned carrying two large Shoo-Fly Pies.

"Here you are, *Melassich Riwwelkuche*," Mary said.

"Oh, I haven't heard Shoo-Fly Pie called that for ages," David said. He shot Mary a winning smile, but she ignored him.

Hannah was relieved to see that Mary appeared to be immune to David's charms, if that was the word for them. As they ate the Shoo-Fly Pie, Hannah could not help but shoot him a furious gaze from time to time, but he simply smirked at her in response.

Her sisters were watching the exchange, and Hannah knew she would have to answer their questions later. Still, she was grateful, as she knew she had their unspoken support.

"I sat up for longer today," Esther announced. "My back doesn't hurt as much."

"Wunderbar," Mr. Miller said. "And how were you today, Martha?"

"Getting there," Martha mumbled, trying to eat with her left hand.

"And how was your first day working for Mrs. Hostetler, Hannah?"

"*Gut, Datt*. I enjoyed it." *That is, until I saw Noah Hostetler*, Hannah silently added.

Hannah's *mudder* muttered under her breath, but it was David who spoke up. "You're working for Mrs. Hostetler!" he exclaimed. His tone was accusatory.

"David." Just the one calmly spoken word from Mr. Miller caused David to go silent, but tension at once descended over the room.

After everyone ate the Shoo-Fly Pies, Mrs. Miller produced pumpkin custard pies.

Hannah usually loved pumpkin custard pies, but the tension hung heavily over the table. After everyone had finished, Mr. Miller addressed David. "David, we would normally invite you to stay for a game of Scrabble, but it's time for my *dochders* go to sleep, and they are living downstairs now, as you can see."

David thanked the Millers and said his goodbyes. His expression was still surly. After David left, Mrs. Miller turned to Mary. "Hannah will help me clean up tonight. You go and get some sleep."

As soon as Mary was out of earshot, Mrs. Miller asked Hannah, "Did you enjoy the dinner with David tonight?"

Hannah knew her *mudder* wouldn't be happy with her answer. "*Mamm*, I have no interest in David."

Her *mudder* turned to her, surprised. "Hannah, you're not getting any younger. David's a good man."

A chill ran up the back of Hannah's spine. "But, *Mamm*, I'm not in love with him."

Mrs. Miller snorted rudely. "Love? Lots of men and women aren't in love when they marry. They grow to love each other. If it's in *Gott's* will, it works out well between them, and then the *bopplin* come along."

Hannah shuddered at the thought, a fact that was not lost on her *mudder.*

Mrs. Miller turned her back to Hannah and banged some pans around. "David is a wealthy man from a wealthy family, and bills will be taken care of if you marry him. It will take a burden from us."

Burden? That's how Mamm *sees me?* Hannah bit her lip and did her best not to burst into tears. It was so unfair. She hadn't caused the accident; she was the victim. There was no way she was going to marry David Yoder. The very thought made her cringe. Even if she had to sit up half the night making quilts to sell in Mrs. Hostetler's store, along with all her other duties, it would be worth it to avoid such an unpleasant situation. Besides, her *mudder* could not force her to marry David Yoder, and she was sure her *daed* was on her side. After all, her *daed* had always approved of Noah Hostetler.

Noah. The very thought of him caused Hannah's heart to race. Today was the first time they had spoken after the accident. He had visited her in the hospital more than once, but each time she had shut her eyes until she heard him leave the room. Tears had pricked her eyes each time when he had again and again poured forth his heartfelt apology. She simply could not open her eyes and face the man who had caused such harm. Her previous feelings for him only made the situation so much worse.

Hannah lay on the mattress that night, unable to

sleep. Hannah had assumed that her old feelings for Noah had left, but seeing him again today had made her doubt that. Even thinking about him now, her heart yearned for him, much to her dismay. “Don’t be so stupid,” she said aloud to herself, and then put her hand over her mouth when Esther stirred.

There was no doubt about it. Whatever future there might have been with Noah Hostetler had been destroyed the day he ran into their buggy.

Chapter Nine

The next morning, Hannah awoke with a start. Someone was shaking her. She sat bolt upright. "Mary, what's happened?"

"I'm sorry to wake you, Hannah, but there was a noise outside my door. At first I thought it was the wind because it was my first night in the house and I didn't know what sort of noises there would be. So I thought it was the wind. I thought maybe the noise was a tree's branches brushing against the house, but then I heard a sound like an animal. I wondered if there was a horse nearby, but I hadn't noticed a horse nearby when I was cleaning the house with your mother. Besides, horses don't make scratching sounds on doors."

Hannah rubbed her eyes. It was too early in the morning and she hadn't had any *kaffi*. She wished Mary would come to the point.

Mary was still speaking. "So I pulled the quilt over my head, but I could still hear the sound like something scratching on the door. Eventually, I got out of bed, and guess what I found?"

"What did you find?" Hannah asked urgently.

"Well, it was a surprise to me, I can tell you," Mary said.

It took every last bit of Hannah's patience not to yell, "Out with it!"

"It was a dog."

"A dog?" Hannah said in shock. "There was a dog outside your door?" Surely she hadn't heard her properly.

"Yes, a dog," Mary whispered. "You don't own a dog, do you?"

Hannah shook her head. "*Nee*, *Mamm* doesn't like pets. We always wanted a pet dog or a pet cat or since we were small, but *Mamm* always said we couldn't have one." She abruptly shut her mouth. Mary's ramblings had obviously rubbed off on her. "Where's the dog now?"

"I've got him tied up on the porch."

Hannah struggled to her feet. "Mary, would you mind fetching my coat and I'll go and see."

Minutes later, Hannah and Mary walked to the *grossmammi haus*. There stood the ugliest and tallest dog Hannah had ever seen. He was a strange mustard color with a big black patch over one eye.

"Isn't he cute!" Mary said.

Hannah looked at her askance. "Well, *cute* isn't exactly the word I would choose, but he sure is friendly." The dog almost knocked her down trying to lick her. "I've never seen him about around these parts before."

"Do you think no one owns him?" Mary asked.

Hannah's heart sank at the hopeful note in Mary's voice. "I'm sorry to tell you, but *Mamm* won't let you keep him, if that's what you were hoping."

That was indeed what Mary had been hoping, given by the fallen expression on her face. "Oh," she said in a small voice.

"I'm sure we'll find his owner," Hannah said. "Mary, could you lead him to the barn and we'll tie him there where it's warm and get him some food and water."

Mary nodded enthusiastically. "I found some of this rope under the kitchen sink. Wasn't that good! Imagine finding rope under the kitchen sink. It would normally be something that was out in the barn, but if it hadn't been under the kitchen sink, what would I have done? There would have been nothing I could have tied up the dog with and he might've gotten away."

Hannah simply nodded. "Perhaps a passing tourist lost him. The poor thing—his ribs are sticking out."

They had reached the barn, and Mary rubbed the dog's head. "No wonder he's cold. There's nothing on his bones to keep him warm."

"I'll stay here with him, Mary, if you could go to the house and fetch some food for him."

"What sort of food will I fetch him?" Mary asked, clearly worried. "I don't want to take the wrong food and upset your *mudder*."

Hannah shook her head. "*Mamm* doesn't like pets, but only because she thinks they're too much trouble. She certainly wouldn't begrudge the hungry dog. Go and fetch some meat. *Mamm* won't mind, truly. I'd fetch it myself if it wasn't for this cast."

"Will I leave the lantern here for you?" Mary asked her.

"*Nee*, you take it. I know my way around."

While Mary was gone, Hannah fetched some water for the dog. She was cold, with only her woollen coat over her nightgown. She pulled it around her tightly and spoke to the dog. "If only you could talk. You must have a story to tell. I haven't seen a dog like you before, and certainly not such a tall one. You look like one of those fancy breeds that the *Englischers* have. What's your name?"

"Pirate," Mary said behind her. "I've named him Pirate. I know it's a very *Englisch* name, but…" Her voice trailed away.

"I think it suits him," Hannah said with a chuckle.

Mary put a large piece of meat down on the ground in front of the dog and he ate it in one gulp. "He sure was hungry," she said.

"We will give him some more after we have *kaffi*." Hannah could almost smell the *kaffi*. She wasn't used to doing so much of a morning before *kaffi*. "If he's been hungry for a long time, we could make him sick by giving him too much food at once. Now let's go inside and make a nice strong pot of *kaffi*."

"Do you think he'll be all right by himself?" Mary asked her.

"We've tied him in this stall, so even if he did manage to untie himself, even a dog of his height wouldn't be able to get out of this stall," Hannah reassured her. "Besides, it's warm in here and he looks quite comfortable." Sure enough, the tall mustard-colored dog had settled down on a large pile of straw.

"What's going to happen to him?" Mary asked.

Hannah shrugged. "We'll have to ask around and find out who owns him."

"What if no one owns him?" Mary said.

"We'll have to find him a good home in that case," Hannah said. "Now let's get that pot of *kaffi* on."

As they walked toward the house, the first shards of dawn light were making their way over the distant hills. Hannah always loved this time of day. It was the peacefulness, and a feeling of anticipation that something good was about to happen.

"I have *kaffi oats* every day at home," Mary said hopefully.

Hannah stopped walking. "*Kaffi oats?* What on earth is that?"

"You make oats, but instead of milk, you use coffee."

Hannah tried to picture it with some difficulty. "Let me see. You make oats, but instead of any milk, you pour on *kaffi*. So you make the *kaffi* first, and then boil the oats in it?"

Mary nodded. "You should try it. It's delicious."

Hannah had her doubts about that. "All right, you make some and I'll try a spoonful, but I'm sure I like my *kaffi* in liquid form."

Mary laughed. Hannah was grateful for the company, and also for the help. Mary insisted Hannah sit at the old oak kitchen table, while she busied herself making a big pot of *kaffi* and then boiling oats in the brewed *kaffi*.

"Should I make some *kaffi oats* for anyone else in the house?" she asked Hannah.

Hannah laughed. "*Nee*, I don't think so." She looked up as one of her sisters slowly walked into the room. "I'm sorry, did we wake you, Esther?"

"Yes," Esther said tactlessly. "I had a strange dream where you two were talking about a dog. Was that real?"

"*Jah*, a dog scratched at the *grossmammi haus* door and woke up Mary this morning," Hannah told her.

Esther's face lit up. "A dog? A real dog? Where is it now?"

"We tied him up in the barn and gave him some food," Hannah said.

Esther clasped her hands in delight. "You think we can keep him?"

Hannah sighed. "*Nee*, you know what *Mamm* is like about pets."

Esther nodded slowly. "Yes. Could he be from one of the neighbouring farms?"

Hannah shook her head. "I've never seen him before and I think I know all the dogs in the district. He doesn't look like a usual farm dog."

"His name is Pirate," Mary supplied. "He has a patch over one eye. Years ago when I was growing up, an *Englisch* family moved in next door, and there was a girl there about my own age, Isabel. She always told me about pirates. They wore a black patch over one eye and had a parrot sitting on their shoulder and they looked for buried treasure and shot other ships with cannons."

When she paused for breath, Hannah spoke. "This dog certainly has a big black patch over his eye, but he doesn't have a parrot on his shoulder."

Mary burst out laughing. She turned to Esther. "I was telling Hannah about *kaffi oats*. Have you ever heard of it?"

"Nee," Esther said, gently lowering herself into a chair. "What is it?"

As Mary explained *kaffi oats* to Esther, who did not look at all keen on the idea, Hannah's thoughts drifted away to the dog. She had always wanted a dog, but her mother had always been vehemently opposed to pets. When Hannah got married, the first thing she intended to do was get a dog.

Married. There was that word. Would Hannah ever get married? Her heart belonged to Noah—or it once did, in days distant past. Could she ever love another?

Chapter Ten

When the taxi deposited Hannah a little way from Mrs. Hostetler's quilt store later that morning, Hannah was caught in a downpour of rain. Although she was wearing her sturdy boot on the leg without a cast, she slipped in a puddle. One of her crutches flew from her hand, but Hannah managed to steady herself against the window of the store. Hannah retrieved her crutch readily enough, but by now she was already drenched.

As Hannah walked through the door to the quilt store, Katie let out a gasp. "Hannah! You must be drenched right through to the bone. Go into the back room at once and get warm."

Hannah did as she was told. Katie hurried after her and turned up the electric fire. "Here, give me your coat." She arranged Hannah's coat over a chair near the fire. "Now take off your boot."

"It's not too bad," Hannah protested.

"Nonsense! I heard it squelching as you walked in."

Hannah had to laugh. She handed Katie her boot and Katie placed it in front of the fire. "I think it's going to take a while to dry," Katie said.

"Maybe I could do my sewing in here," Hannah offered.

Katie shot her a smile. "*Jah*, that's a good idea. But you won't do anything until you have a nice cup of mint tea to warm you up."

Hannah was soon feeling somewhat warmed, her hands wrapped around the hot mug of mint tea. Her toes were cold, so she hoped her boot would dry soon. It wasn't terribly wet, but damp enough to cause a cold if she were to put it back on now.

"We found a dog at our house this morning," Hannah said by way of conversation. "Do you know anyone who has lost a dog? He's tall and a funny brown color with a black patch over one eye. He's quite distinctive looking."

Katie shook her head. "*Nee*, I haven't heard anyone missing a dog, but I'll ask around."

"Denki," Hannah said. "*Mamm* was quite shocked when we told her this morning. I'm sure Mary would like to keep him, but *Mamm* is very set in her ways about having pets." Hannah looked up to see Katie frowning. No doubt Katie thought Mrs. Miller was set in her ways about more than just pets.

"It must be a help having Mary there," Katie said.

Hannah agreed enthusiastically. "Yes, she's such a help, and with me sitting down rather than walking around, I'm certain my leg will improve quickly."

"I'm sure it will," Katie said. "It's time to open the store, so will you be all right by yourself?"

Hannah said she would.

"I'll fetch you some sewing to do." Katie soon returned with some colorful fabric, and said, "Here you are, Hannah. Here are some puzzle balls for you to sew."

Hannah took the fabric from her. *"Denki."*

"Just come out as soon as your clothes dry." With that, Katie left. Hannah sewed for a while and then checked her boot. It was toasty warm so she put it back on. Her sock was another matter. While it was certainly no longer drenched, it was still wet, so she pushed it as close to the fire as she did. If only she could wear stockings again, but the cast made that impossible. She turned her coat around to warm the other side.

Hannah did not like sewing in the back room. For one, the view was only of the four walls and they were not particularly interesting. Sure, it was warm, but sitting in the store was never boring, not with customers popping in and out. On her first day, Hannah sat at the back wall, affording her a view of one section of this street. It made sewing pass by in an interesting manner.

What's more, she was still a little uncomfortable working in the store. While she liked Katie well enough, Katie was Noah's mother after all, and that very fact made Hannah uncomfortable. She was no longer afraid that Noah would come to the store, not after his mother's reaction to him the other day.

She was sure Katie had given Noah a thorough lecture after his previous visit, so he wasn't likely to do that again.

Hannah tried to deny the fact that somewhere deep inside her, she wanted Noah to come back to the store, and was disappointed that he wouldn't. The small hope arose that he might, and she was annoyed with herself for allowing herself that hope. What was wrong with her? She was on crutches all because of Noah. Rebecca was in the hospital all because of Noah. Her sisters had back injuries because of Noah, and her parents were in a tight financial situation because of Noah. How could she entertain any thoughts of him?

Hannah shook her head and turned her attention to her sewing. It was just not right. No, she would have to move on. Noah could not be in her future, even if some part of her wanted him to be. She would have to find another man to marry. She knew that man certainly wouldn't be David, and as nice as John was, it wouldn't be him either. Still, that was no reason to despair because there were more men in the world than David and John.

She sighed aloud. Yes, there were more men in the world. Still, she firmly held the common Amish belief that there is one man for every woman and one woman for every man. She sent up a silent prayer to *Gott* that he would bring her husband to her.

Hannah tested her sock again and it was dry. She sighed with relief. There was too much opportunity for introspection sitting in the small room with no view. She put on her sock and boot, and then pulled on her wool coat, tucked the puzzle balls under her arm and opened the door to the store.

Hannah could hear a woman talking. She opened the door to the store and as she did, she remembered she had left some fabric behind. She hobbled back to the table and tucked it under her arm as well.

As she turned to walk back in, she heard the woman say, "It's good that Noah has found himself a girl. I thought he would never get over Hannah Miller."

Hannah heard Katie's sharp intake of breath—or maybe it was her own.

The woman looked up to see Katie standing in the doorway. She gasped, excused herself and hurried out the door. Hannah recognized her as Mrs. Lapp, one of the widows in the community.

Katie turned to Hannah. "Mrs. Lapp is quite mistaken." Her face flushed beet red and she seemed to be struggling for words. "Noah doesn't have a girlfriend. I don't know what Mrs. Lapp was thinking."

Hannah wondered what to say next, but could not find the words, so she merely nodded and walked over to her table and chair. She put down the puzzle balls and fabric and bent her head over the one she was working on, furiously sewing.

Out of the corner of her eye, Hannah could see Katie looking at her for a while, but then another customer came in, an *Englischer.* Katie was soon consumed showing the English lady the quilts and the customer was deciding between buying two of them.

Hannah was grateful for the distraction. Katie wouldn't see the tears rolling down her cheeks. Mrs. Lapp wasn't a gossip, so she had heard that from someone or had seen it with her own eyes. The fact that Katie didn't know was surely irrelevant. Mrs. Lapp wouldn't have made that up. Maybe Noah didn't want his mother to know and was keeping it from her.

Hannah dug her fingernails into her palm to try to stop crying, but it didn't help. She was angry with herself for being so upset that Noah had moved on.

That afternoon, Hannah visited Rebecca as usual, and on this occasion, a young nurse was talking to Rebecca when Hannah entered the room. The nurse made to leave, but paused at the door and looked back at the two. "Rebecca, you have so many visitors that you'll be sad to go home. You'll miss them, I bet, especially the four handsome young men." With that, the nurse winked at Rebecca and then left.

Four handsome young men? Hannah thought. She looked at Rebecca and saw that she was decidedly uncomfortable, squirming in her bed. Then it dawned on her. The young men must be the four Hostetler brothers, Noah, Jacob, Moses, and Elijah. Her stomach churned and the room spun.

"Hannah, you've gone white. Sit down on my bed or in the chair."

Hannah sat on the edge of Rebecca's bed and struggled to control her breathing. After the accident, the psychologist had told her that anxiety could be managed by long, slow breaths. *Four breaths in, hold for two counts, four breaths out*, she silently told herself.

Hannah sat for a while, breathing in a controlled manner, and then opened her eyes to see Rebecca peering at her with worry stamped all over her face.

"When," she stammered, "when have they been visiting you?"

"Mostly in the mornings." Rebecca's voice was small and flat. "You always come in the afternoons and they come in the mornings."

Hannah shook her head. She didn't want to begrudge her sister visitors. She knew only too well what it was like to lie in a hospital bed for weeks. Yet the Hostetlers, of all people?

Rebecca broke the silence. "Hannah, it's not of *Gott's* way to hold anger in your heart. Besides, Noah was the one responsible, not his *bruders* or his *mudder* or his *vadder*."

Hannah did not trust herself to speak, so just sat there. Finally she said, "But Rebecca, *Datt* and *Mamm* will be angry when they find out. Whatever will they say? Sure, okay, I can understand the rest of his *familye*, but Noah Hostetler himself visiting you?" She shook her head.

"They won't mind, Hannah." Rebecca's tone was insistent.

Hannah sighed. "Yes, they will most certainly mind if they find out."

"No, they won't. Oh Hannah, I'm not supposed to tell you, but…" Her voice trailed away and she fidgeted nervously.

"What? Come on, Rebecca, you can't say that and then not tell me."

Rebecca pulled a face and chewed on a fingernail. "*Datt* was going to tell you when the time was right, but, but..." Rebecca took one look at Hannah's face and then continued. "They already know."

"They already know that Noah Hostetler and his *bruders* are visiting you?"

Rebecca nodded.

"They do?" Hannah was puzzled. She figured her *daed* would likely be fine with it, but certainly not their *mudder*. Just the mention of the name *Hostetler* was enough to cause their *mudder* to go into a pot-banging outburst. Hannah looked at Rebecca and saw that she was still chewing a fingernail. "There's more, isn't there?"

Rebecca nodded. "I wasn't supposed to say. Don't be angry, Hannah, but Noah is working for *Datt*."

"Working for *Datt*?" Hannah repeated loudly as a chill ran down her spine. "Whatever do you mean?"

"He's working for *Datt* in his furniture store, as a furniture maker."

"Noah Hostetler is making furniture for our *vadder*?" Hannah clenched her fists to try to stop the lightheaded sensation that was threatening to overtake her. "But, if he's making furniture rather than selling it in the store, that means he's making in *Datt's* workshop, at home, behind our *haus*."

Rebecca nodded.

Hannah stood up and hobbled to the window on her crutches. She looked down at the people scurrying this way and that as if they didn't have a care in the world. "This means Noah's been there when I've been at home and no one's told me," she said aloud, but to herself.

"Come and sit down, Hannah. *Datt* was waiting for the right time to tell you," Rebecca said again.

How could he? How could my own daed *keep that from me?* she wondered. *Noah Hostetler, the very one who caused all of us to have injuries for many weeks, and* Datt *not only forgives him, but gives him a job.* Hannah's whole face was burning. Even her ears felt as though they were on fire.

"*Gott* wants us to forgive," Rebecca pressed, but Hannah was in a daze. Rebecca raised her voice slightly. "Judge not, and ye shall not be judged: condemn not, and ye shall not be condemned: forgive, and ye shall be forgiven."

Hannah gasped. "Rebecca! You mustn't do that; people will call you *Scripture smart.*" Hannah felt a pang of sympathy when she looked at Rebecca's fallen face. "Anyway, you sound like *Datt,*" she added in a teasing voice.

Rebecca brightened up.

Chapter Eleven

Hannah had the taxi stop at her *daed's* workshop rather than at the *haus* as usual. She had not been to the workshop since her accident. It was behind the barn, so not visible from their house, and had another entryway. No wonder she hadn't seen Noah drive his buggy past.

The bishop had long ago given Mr. Miller permission to have electricity and a computer in his workshop, as well as a phone in the barn, due to the fact that the woodworking business was the Millers' sole source of income. Mr. Miller had purchased the small property from *Englischers* after he decided to sell his farm and go into the woodworking business. While all electrical lines had been pulled out of the *haus* and the barn, the bishop allowed the electrical lines to remain to the big building that Mr. Miller was to use as his workshop.

Hannah hobbled to the workshop, wondering why she hadn't seen a buggy out there, but then realized that Noah would have unhitched his horse and put him on the other side of the barn, and left the buggy out the back.

Hannah struggled to push the door open and then made her way inside slowly. Both her *daed* and Noah saw her at the same time. She would have laughed at the shocked and stricken expressions on their faces if this hadn't been such a serious matter. After all, her father had betrayed her by keeping the matter from her.

"*Datt*, can I speak with you for a moment, please?"

Her father hurried over. "Are your *schweschders* all right? Is anything wrong?"

"*Nee*, they're fine. I just want to talk with you."

Mr. Miller nodded to Noah to continue. Hannah tried not to look at him, but couldn't help noticing his face was white. Noah went to the back of the workshop and turned on a noisy piece of equipment, presumably to give Hannah and her *daed* an opportunity to speak without being overheard.

Hannah sat in her father's small office. "*Datt*, I heard that Noah's working for you! I've heard he's been working for you for some time."

"*Jah*, that's right, he has. I didn't want to tell you until the time was right."

Hannah studied her *daed's* face. He didn't look remorseful or embarrassed at all. "But what right time? When would that time be?"

Mr. Miller patted her hand. "I was going to tell you when you had forgiven Noah."

"Forgiven!" Hannah said the word loudly and then

looked up at Noah, but was certain he hadn't heard her over the noise of the loud equipment.

"*Jah*. Hannah, you know that *Gott* wants you to forgive; you must. Why do you hold such hatred in your heart?"

Tears pricked the corner of Hannah's eyes. "I don't hate Noah. But how can I forgive him after what he did to me? To my *schweschders*? How can you forgive him, *Datt*?"

"I forgave him through the Grace of *Gott*, and so must you, *dochder*."

Tears were falling from Hannah's eyes now. "But how?"

"Ask *Gott* to help you, child. Many things we cannot do on our own strength, so we have to rest on the strength of *Gott*. Would you like to speak to the bishop?"

"Nee, Datt!" Hannah struggled to her feet. Why did her *daed* have to bring the bishop into it? Anyone would think that Hannah had committed a sin, when she was the victim. Well, unforgiveness was a sin, she knew that, but how could she forgive? And she had expected her father to be remorseful and apologetic, but instead, he had lectured her.

"I'll go and help *Mamm* with dinner now, *Datt*."

As Hannah made her way to the door, her *daed* called out after her, "Tell your *mudder* that Noah will be coming for dinner tonight."

Hannah froze in her tracks. Things were going from bad to worse. It was like a nightmare and she was unable to wake up.

* * *

Noah had been shocked to see Hannah come through the door to the workshop, asking to speak with her *vadder*. He figured Hannah must have just found out that he was working for him. She sure did not look pleased about it. And even worse, Mr. Miller had informed Noah that he was to come to dinner. It had been a summons rather than an invitation.

It was bad enough that Noah would have to sit at the same table with Mrs. Miller, whom he had no doubt would be shooting angry glances and perhaps even words his way, but he couldn't bear to see Hannah's accusing eyes on him all the time, not when he harbored such deep feelings for her.

Noah walked outside the workshop and over to Rock. He climbed through the rails to straighten Rock's winter blanket. "Why do you always need your blanket straightened, Rock?" he asked the horse as he gave him a handful of oats. "Is it because you know that I'll give you a handful of oats when I fix it?"

Noah rubbed Rock's face. "I'm sorry, old boy. It's my fault you're like this. I bet you're missing all the attention of being a buggy horse and going out visiting. It's all my fault."

Hannah stood outside the workshop, her face to the sky. The snowflakes drifted through the icy air and settled on her face. Noah Hostetler was working for her *daed*. How could this be so? She shook her head, scattering the snowflakes.

It was one thing to have to sit through a whole dinner with Noah, but worse still, she would have to be the one to tell her *mudder* that he would be coming for dinner.

Hannah was annoyed with her *daed* for forgiving Noah, and knew that her *mudder* felt the same way. Her *mudder* would be upset that Mr. Miller had invited Noah for dinner, and Hannah was sure that her *mudder* did not approve of the fact that Noah had been working for her *daed*. That was obviously what their recent conversation had been about.

The cold drove Hannah on toward the *haus*, so she made her way carefully, reluctant to face her *mudder*.

When Hannah finally did tell Mrs. Miller that Noah was coming for dinner, her *mudder* simply said with narrowed eyes and pursed lips, "So you know he's been working for your *daed*?"

Hannah nodded.

Her *mudder* thumped around the kitchen, muttering to herself and banging pots and pans, as Hannah knew she would. Hannah rested her crutches against the wall, balanced herself on her plaster cast, and then busied herself mashing the potatoes. Her *mudder* was still muttering as Hannah added cream cheese to the potatoes, mashed again, and then added butter and sour cream. As she stirred, she remembered the times she had thought she would one day be cooking for Noah, as his *fraa*. Well, Noah had wasted no time finding someone else, according to Mrs. Lapp.

"Hmpf!" she said aloud, drawing her *mudder's* attention.

"Is your leg hurting, Hannah?"

"Nee, Mamm." Hannah was embarrassed that she'd let her feelings show to the extent of speaking, or rather, snorting loudly. She had better not speak her thoughts out aloud tonight over the dinner table with Noah there.

Noah! Just the thought of his name made Hannah's knees go weak. Once she had been deeply in love with him, but now… Well, she didn't know what she felt any more. Perhaps old habits died hard. Maybe what she still felt for Noah was just a habit. It couldn't be love, surely? Not after everything he had done to her and her *familye.* Hannah's eyes fell to her crutches, and she set her shoulders square with resolve. *I am not in love with Noah Hostetler*, she told herself. *Maybe I should consider John, after all. He didn't seem so bad. It's time for me to move on. Noah certainly has.*

When Mr. Miller and Noah came through the front door, it seemed to Hannah that Noah was quite wary. *And so he should be, what with* Mamm *here*, she thought. Noah smiled at her and she smiled back automatically, but then she frowned. His smile always could light her up. And why did her heart flutter every time she saw him? *Oh* Gott, *please help me not to be so conflicted*, she said silently.

The *familye* and Noah all bowed their heads in the silent prayer, and when Hannah opened her eyes, she could almost see the frost that had descended upon the table. It had nothing to do with the weather, and all to do with her *mudder.* Even the delightful aroma of chicken and gravy did nothing to lighten the atmosphere.

Mr. Miller did not seem to notice, and talked as he usually did. He spoke often to Noah, no doubt to put him at ease, as Mrs. Miller was avoiding talking to him and often shot glares his way.

"How's Jacob?" Esther piped up.

Noah looked up, seemingly surprised that someone other than Mr. Miller had spoken to him. Hannah felt a momentary pang of sympathy for him.

"He's *gut, denki.* He's always asking after you. Please tell me exactly how you are so I can tell him."

Esther smiled widely. "My back's much better now. I'm sitting up for longer and longer periods and it doesn't hurt much at all now," she gushed. "Soon I'll be around and about, helping *Mamm* again."

Hannah knew that Esther had always been sweet on Jacob, and clearly the accident hadn't changed that. *Oh well, he wasn't the one who was driving,* she thought. *Esther can't hold Jacob accountable for his* bruder's *sins.*

Hannah saw Esther shoot a glance at their *mudder.* "It would be good if Jacob could visit," Esther added in a nervous voice.

"Esther!" Mrs. Miller's voice was loud. Everyone turned to look at her, except for Mr. Miller.

"*Jah*, that's a *gut* idea." Mr. Miller's voice was firm.

Now everyone turned to look at Mr. Miller.

"A *gut* idea," he repeated, with slightly more

emphasis. He ignored his *fraa's* glares and continued speaking. "Esther and Martha must be bored with just lying around all day and unable to do their chores. Idle hands are no good."

Hannah saw him look at their *mudder's* face and then look back to Noah.

Mrs. Miller cleared her throat. "Hannah."

Everyone looked at Mrs. Miller and then at Hannah.

"You know that Mary Knepp has taken ill?" Her voice was cold and a little angry.

Hannah wondered at the abrupt change of subject. "*Jah, Mamm*. How is she?"

"The *doktor* said it's a case of the flu and that she has to rest up for a couple weeks."

Hannah made to murmur sympathetically, but her *mudder* cut her off.

"That means there's no one to teach the *kinner* at school."

Hannah was taken aback. "But, *Mamm*, I can't do that."

Mrs. Miller waved her hand through the air. "*Nee*, Hannah," she said sharply. "I don't mean you should teach them."

Hannah breathed a sigh of relief, but wondered where this conversation was going. She didn't have a good feeling about it, and sensed her mother was up to something.

She didn't have long to wait, as Mrs. Miller wasted no time speaking again. "Beth Yoder will teach them until Mary's well again, but Beth has never taught *kinner* before, and she's asked for your help."

Aha, Hannah thought, *Beth Yoder, David's* mudder. *This is all part of* Mamm's *matchmaking plot. It seems Beth Yoder might be in on it, too.* Her heart sank. It was bad enough that she had to deal with her feelings for Noah, whatever they were. Now she had to fend off the unpleasant David Yoder. Not only that, her own *mudder*, and now David's mother, Beth, were trying to get them together.

"Hannah?" Her *mudder's* tone was insistent.

"Oh sorry, *Mamm.*" Hannah saw that everyone around the table was looking at her, particularly Noah, who was staring, waiting for her response.

She licked her lips nervously. "*Mamm*, I can't, really. I visit Rebecca in the hospital every day, and do the chores here as much as I can, and I help Mrs. Hostetler in the store three mornings a week."

"I'm sure Mrs. Hostetler can do without you."

Mr. Miller interrupted. "*Nee*. Hannah is to continue to work for Mrs. Hostetler. It wouldn't be right to abandon her like that."

Mrs. Miller looked down at the table. "Well then, Hannah, you can help Mrs. Yoder on the other two mornings."

Hannah looked at her *daed*, hoping he would protest, but to her dismay he remained silent this time.

Mrs. Miller stood up to clear the dishes. "It will only be for a week or two before Mary is well again. You can start next week."

"Jah, Mamm," Hannah said meekly.

"*Gut*, Beth will be pleased. And I'm sure you're looking forward to seeing David at the Singing this Sunday night."

"David?" *I really should think before I speak,* Hannah thought, *but what can I say to that without getting into trouble? Nothing*, she decided, so said aloud, "*Nee*, *Mamm*, I am not."

Esther and Martha gasped at Hannah's boldness, but Hannah thought that her *daed's* eyes twinkled. Mrs. Miller appeared to be too angry to speak. Her jaw opened and shut. Hannah felt Noah's eyes on her and looked up. He held her gaze until she looked away.

Esther spoke up. "Can I go to the Singing please, *Mamm*?"

Hannah shot Esther a grateful look. She knew Esther had no desire to go the Singing with her bad back, but was merely deflecting attention away from Hannah.

Mrs. Miller shook her head. "Not yet, Esther, but I'm sure you and Martha will be well enough to go soon."

Hannah was in two minds about the Singing. Noah and David would both be there. She couldn't shake the feeling that an awkward situation was looming.

Noah sighed long and deep to himself as he drove his buggy home in the dark. The dinner had been difficult and strained, and the worst thing of all was that Mrs. Miller was trying to set up his beloved Hannah with David Yoder. Hannah had not appeared keen on the idea, but was she only being coy? Noah had no way of knowing. Being so close to Hannah for an evening had made his heart ache more than ever.

Chapter Twelve

That day, the church and the Singing were to be held in the Lapps' barn. The Lapps' *haus* was very small and could not accommodate the community, whereas their barn was quite large. For that reason, the community held the church meeting and the Singing in the Lapps' barn when it was the Lapps' turn to have both. Unlike most Amish homes, which had been built to hold large groups of people, theirs was a tiny *Grossdawdi Haus* that the Lapps' only son had purchased, along with his own adjoining *haus*, from *Englischers* some years ago. When their son had been tragically killed in a buggy accident, the Lapps had sold off his home, but kept its parcel of land with the barn.

"I wish I could come," Martha lamented over breakfast that morning.

"Me, too." Esther pushed a bit of cornmeal around with her spoon in her *scrapple*.

Hannah felt sorry for them. "You'll both soon be

coming, too. In fact, you'll be wishing you hadn't when you have to sit through one of Mr. Petersheim's long talks on hell," she added, hoping that Mr. Petersheim wouldn't be one of the ministers speaking that day.

Esther and Martha laughed while their *mudder* frowned and opened her mouth to rebuke Hannah. "Hannah!" she said. "That's enough! You could certainly do with a talk on hell!"

Later, in the church service, Hannah tried to keep her balance on the backless, wooden bench with her leg in its cast stuck out in front of her, listening to none other than Mr. Petersheim giving a lengthy sermon in a monotone voice. He was preaching on *hochmut*, pride, this time, but he had gone on for an hour longer than any other minister usually did. This was supposed to be the *short* sermon too; a long one would follow it. Hannah wondered if *Gott* was punishing her for being so disrespectful earlier.

Hannah looked around the barn. *Nothing's changed*, she thought. *It all looks the same.* The last time she was in this barn was a year ago, months before the accident. If only she'd known then what would happen to her. Hannah shook her head in an attempt to clear it of such fanciful thoughts.

Hannah looked at Mr. Petersheim, but he was still walking around and speaking about pride in a loud voice. She looked around the barn, and then at the beams way above her head. *It would be hard to keep such a large place clean*, she thought idly, *since the Lapps don't use it for farming.*

Hannah's thoughts drifted to Noah. He had nodded and smiled to her when she arrived, and she had nodded back politely. Why did her mouth run dry every time she saw him? Why did she long to run and throw herself into his arms, those big strong arms? With his arms around her, she was sure she would feel safe. Hannah shook her head. *Have I gone mad? The reason I feel bad in the first place is all because of Noah.*

She sneaked a glance at Noah who was sitting on the other side of the room with all the other single men, but David happened to look up at that point and caught her eye. He smiled broadly and winked at her.

Nee*, now David will think I'm interested in him*, she thought with dismay. *This must be* Gott's *way of telling me to concentrate on the message the minister is bringing us today.* Hannah turned her mind back to the sermon, and tried to concentrate as best she could.

The service finally came to an end, having run for an hour and a half longer than it usually did. Hannah had caught herself yawning during the speaking, and had hoped no one else had noticed.

Usually, people ate in shifts after a church meeting, but as the Lapps' barn was so large, everyone was able to eat the same time, although the men ate at different tables from the women as usual.

The men turned the wooden benches into tables, and the women soon had them laden with plates, refusing Hannah's help. Hannah's mouth watered at the sight of her usual favorite. It was *church spread*, peanut butter spread sweetened with blackstrap molasses and marshmallow crème.

Soon, the women brought in jugs of *kaffi* and water and placed them next to the plates of pickles, cheese, red beet, bread, and *snitz*, dried apple pie.

After they ate, the people mingled with each other. Most of the young people were talking about the night's Singing to come. After a while, Hannah sat down to have a rest; her arms were aching and her leg was hurting. She saw Noah heading in her direction, and hoped he would walk straight past her. However, he did not.

"*Hiya*, Hannah. Are you taking a rest?"

Obviously, I'm taking a rest. I'm not sitting down simply because I find this hard wooden bench so comfortable, Hannah thought unkindly. She bit her lip before answering, *"Jah."* Still, why did her heart flutter so every time she saw Noah? Why did her pulse race?

I hope he leaves now, Hannah thought, feeling awkward sitting there with Noah towering above her.

Noah did not appear to be deterred by Hannah's sharply spoken one-word answer or by her distant manner. "How are you feeling?"

Hannah was pondering how to answer that question politely, when David Yoder appeared and stood next to Noah. "How do you think she's feeling, Noah? How would anyone feel after a car had hit their buggy and broken their leg?"

Hannah gasped. David's tone was not overtly hostile. Rather, he was making an effort to pretend he was speaking in a lighthearted manner, but how could such words ever be said in jest? Never mind the fact that Hannah had been thinking those very words, but no matter what, she would never say them to Noah.

Noah and David faced each other. "David Yoder." Noah said the words politely and nodded his head at David.

To Hannah's mind, David looked disappointed by Noah's reaction. It was obvious to her that David been trying to provoke Noah by his words.

A slow red flush appeared on David's neck and traveled up his cheeks. He reached for Hannah's arm and said, "Come on, Hannah. I'll help you over to one of the gas heaters. It's too cold over here."

Hannah shook off his hand. "*Nee*, David. *Denki*, but I'm in the middle of talking to Noah right now."

Both David and Noah looked equally surprised by her words, but David appeared furious. "All right, then," he all but spat, before hurrying back to the others.

Noah turned to Hannah with a smile on his face, but his smile did not last when Hannah didn't return it. Noah looked at Hannah for a moment, his forehead furrowed in a frown. "Hannah, could I fetch you a mug of *kaffi* to warm you up?"

"*Denki*, Noah. That would be good, but then I want to sit here alone to think and pray."

Noah's face fell. "All right." He dutifully went off to get Hannah a mug of *kaffi*, while Hannah watched for any sign of David Yoder returning. Thankfully he did not, and after Noah gave her the mug of *kaffi*, he too left.

Finally, I'm alone, Hannah thought, albeit wishing she were alone in a warmer spot than this. Yet did she want to be alone? She could not but help respect Noah for the way he had handled David's blatant rudeness. She watched Noah now, speaking with one of the young, pretty girls, and she clenched her teeth until her jaw ached. Is that the girl Mrs. Lapp said he was seeing?

What's wrong with me? she asked herself as she shifted around to try to get comfortable on the seat. *How can I be jealous, when Noah is the very one who did this to me?*

Noah chatted to Susanna, but his mind was on Hannah. He kept glancing over at Hannah, trying not to make it look obvious. He was heartened by the fact she had refused David Yoder's offer to help her walk over to the heaters. *Perhaps she's warming up to me*, he thought, but then shook his head. Nee, *she didn't want to spend any time with me after that.*

Noah sighed and turned to listen to the young woman who was trying to capture his attention, totally oblivious to the fact that Hannah was watching them both, and was doing her best not to be overcome with jealousy.

"*Hullo*, Noah."

He spun around to see Mrs. Lapp, the sister of the man in whose house the church meeting had been held that day.

"*Hullo*, Mrs. Lapp," he said. Susanna walked away with her friends, giggling.

"Oh, I'm sorry to interrupt," Mrs. Lapp said.

Noah shook his head. "*Nee*, you didn't interrupt."

"Well, I'm sure the two of you will have plenty of time to speak with each other later, when you drive her home in your buggy after the Singing."

Noah was utterly perplexed. "I'm not sure what you mean," he said, scratching his head.

It was Mrs. Lapp's turn to look puzzled. "Why, aren't you dating Susanna?"

Noah frowned. "*Nee*. You thought I was dating Susanna?"

Mrs. Lapp's hand flew to her mouth. "I'm so sorry. Of course it should have been a secret."

"I'm not seeing her," Noah said firmly. "Whatever gave you that idea, Mrs. Lapp? I'm not seeing anybody."

Mrs. Lapp frowned hard. "That's strange. Jessie Yoder told me that you were seeing Susanna."

Aha. That made sense. Jessie was David's younger *schweschder*. No doubt David was trying to drive a further wedge between Noah and Hannah. He had enlisted his sister to tell Mrs. Lapp that he was dating someone else, in the hopes the news would get back to Hannah. Aloud he said, "*Nee*, Mrs. Lapp. I can assure you, I'm definitely not dating Susanna."

Mrs. Lapp looked over at the giggling girl. " I'm sure she'd like you to."

Noah shrugged one shoulder. "Be that as it may, I have no interest."

"No wonder your *mudder* looked so surprised when I told her in her store the other day."

Noah's breath caught in his throat and his chest constricted. "You told my *mudder*? In her store?"

Mrs. Lapp nodded. Noah dearly wanted to ask if Hannah had been present at the time, but he felt he could hardly do so.

How did things turn out so badly?

Chapter Thirteen

Mr. Miller drove the buggy home after church. He and Mrs. Miller were speaking to each other, while Mary was chatting away to Hannah in an animated fashion. "Everyone was so nice there."

"That's good," Hannah said. "I'm glad *Mamm* introduced you to everyone. I would have liked to, but I had to sit instead of walking around, of course."

"Yes, of course," Mary said. "Mrs. Miller introduced me to absolutely everyone there. Everyone was so nice. And the message was good, although that minister spoke for a very long time. It's hard when people speak for a very long time, isn't it?" Hannah opened her mouth to speak, but Mary pushed on. "Yes, what he said was good, but if someone speaks for a long time, you tend to switch off, don't you?"

Hannah nodded.

Mary barely drew breath. "And isn't it funny that no one knows who owns Pirate? No one had even seen him and no one knows who owns him. It's very strange."

"He did look as though he'd come from a long way," Hannah said. "He was very thin and his paws were rubbed raw."

Mrs. Miller turned around. "The bishop is going to contact the authorities and tell them about the dog."

Mary gasped. "Are the authorities going to take Pirate away?"

Mrs. Miller narrowed her eyes. "*Nee.* Don't get worked up about it, Mary. We'll find a good temporary home for the dog, and when the owners are found, then they will know just where to look."

"What if the owner is never found," Hannah wondered aloud. "Even though Pirate is huge, he seems to be a puppy. Maybe someone thought they had too many puppies."

"He's hardly a puppy, Hannah," Mrs. Miller said in a scolding tone. "He's almost the size of a horse."

"He is still quite a young dog," Mr. Miller said as he moved the horse off to the side of the road as much as possible as a truck sped past a little too close for comfort. "Don't worry, Mary. We'll find a good temporary home for the dog."

Mary nodded. Hannah knew that Mary would dearly love to keep the dog, but she just as well knew her mother would not allow any pets on the place.

When they got home, Hannah was barely through the door when Esther called out, "How was the meeting? Did you see anyone we know?"

Mrs. Miller made a strangled sound. "We saw *everyone* you know, Esther. What sort of question is that?"

Hannah, of course, knew Esther was referring to Jacob. She signaled to Esther that she would tell her later. She had overheard Jacob asking Mr. Miller how Esther was doing.

"Mary, come and help me with the lunch, and then you can take that dog for a walk before the guests arrive."

"Guests?" Hannah said, hoping it wasn't David.

"John is coming. And so is David," Mrs. Miller said with a smirk. "I invited him when he said he wanted to see the dog."

I bet he did, Hannah thought unkindly.

While Mrs. Miller and Mary were in the kitchen preparing lunch, Hannah went to speak with Esther and Rebecca. "I overheard Jacob asking how you were doing," Hannah told Esther. "He didn't ask how anyone else was doing."

"I'm not offended that he didn't ask after me," Rebecca said. "He's sweet on Esther."

"He is not," Esther said, her cheeks flushing red.

Hannah laughed. "It was a much longer meeting than usual," she added.

"Yes, I was getting worried because you are taking so long," Esther said. "Let me guess, Mr. Petersheim?"

Hannah nodded. "Yes, he did speak for a very long time but his message was *gut*." She rubbed her forehead.

"Are you all right?" Esther asked her.

"*Jah*. Just getting a bit of a headache. I think I'll

go and sit in the garden." Hannah loved to sit in the garden, on a little wooden seat her father had put there when they were children. Her mother kept lavender for medicinal reasons, mostly for headaches, and kept a wide variety of healing herbs such as comfrey, nettle, rosemary, peppermint, milk thistle, goldenseal, valerian, blessed thistle. While her mother employed medicinal herbs on a regular basis, she was nowhere near as skilled as old Mrs. Graber.

Hannah sat on the seat and then leaned down to smell the lavender. Even though it was at the very end of winter, there was still a faint scent of lavender around the bushes. The rosemary still had a pungent fragrance. Fragrance always cheered up Hannah. If she was feeling down in any way, smelling flowers made her feel so much better. "Maybe I'm sensitive to scents," she said aloud to herself. "Maybe that's why having to stay in the hospital was even harder for me."

"Are you talking to yourself?" Mary said.

Hannah swiveled around to see Mary bouncing over to her. "My *Englisch* friend says it's the first sign of madness, you know."

"What is?" Hannah said, alarmed.

Mary laughed. "Don't worry. It's only a joke." She bit her lip, and then added, "At least, I think it is. I'm going to get Pirate and take him for a walk. Mrs. Miller said I have time to take him for a short walk before David Yoder and John arrive for lunch."

Hannah's nose crinkled at the sound of David's name.

Mary hurried over to the barn and soon came

back with Pirate. "You know, I think he's put on weight already."

Hannah stared at the dog. "You're right. And now his coat has a bit of a shine to it."

Just then they heard the sound of a buggy and soon David's buggy rounded the corner. "It's David Yoder," Hannah said. "Looks like you won't have time for your walk."

"That won't matter," Mary said cheerfully. "I'll take Pirate for a walk later. At least he's getting some attention."

David tied up his horse and then hurried over to the women while his horse snorted and stared at Pirate. "What a lovely dog," he gushed. "He's so tall! I had no idea he was so big."

"His name is Pirate," Mary told him.

David laughed. "Pirate?"

"Yes," Mary said firmly. She narrowed her eyes.

"What a good name. It suits him."

Hannah was watching the exchange. Was David putting on a good act? He was certainly nicer than usual.

"It's funny that no one in the community has ever seen him or knows anything of him," Mary told David. "He was very thin when he arrived, but he's already put on some weight and Hannah can even see a shine in his coat. I can, too. He's very friendly. I'd love to keep him, only Mrs. Miller doesn't like pets and I don't know how long I'll be living here so I can hardly send him back home. If only I could send him back home with John. If John had driven his buggy here, I could, only you'd never be able to drive a buggy that distance, so we had to hire a driver. I don't imagine John would like going back in a taxi with a huge dog sitting next to him all that way. Besides, do taxis even allow dogs in them? They probably don't. It's probably against some law somewhere to have a big dog in a taxi." Mary finally stopped to draw breath.

"I've always wanted my own dog," David said. He was looking at the dog while he spoke. "When I was a baby, my parents got a puppy, Patches, but he died years ago. He was fifteen at the time. I'd love to have Pirate."

Mary gasped. "You? You want to keep Pirate? What if the owner comes for him?"

"Of course I will have to hand him over to his owners in that case," David said, "but if the owners never turn up, I'd love to have a dog like Pirate."

Pirate certainly liked David. He spent some time licking David's hand and now was scratching his ear on David's knee. David crouched down and put his arms around the dog's neck.

Hannah wondered if David was being genuine, or if he was only pretending to like the dog. And if so, for what purpose? She found it all quite puzzling.

"When would you take him home with you?" Mary said.

"After lunch, if the Millers allow me," David said.

Mary crossed her arms over her chest. "I was hoping no one would look after him and so he would have to stay here and I could look after him longer."

"*Mamm* wouldn't allow that," Hannah told her. "She probably intended to find a home for the dog today." David shot her a grateful look but she merely glared at him. She was not saying that for David's benefit; she was saying it for Mary's. Mary and the dog had to be parted at some time, and the sooner the better for Mary's sake.

"You can come and visit him at any time," David said to Mary.

"That means I have to speak to you," Mary said.

Hannah felt her jaw open in shock.

David appeared equally surprised. "I'm not sure what you mean," he said.

"I mean no offense," Mary began, "but you seem a rather unpleasant person to be around. I notice you're arrogant and have a high opinion of yourself. I'm surprised you like animals. Do you have another motive for taking Pirate? Do you hope Hannah will visit you to see him? I'm telling you now, Hannah likes Pirate, but she has no special attachment to him. I'm the one with the special attachment to him."

David appeared to be so shocked he didn't know what to say. He was struck silent. "Um, um," he sputtered.

"I don't mean any offense," Mary added cheerily. "My mother says I should think before I speak. I do try to, but the words just keep coming out and I don't seem to be able to stop them. You do seem to be nice to animals, even though you're not nice to people." With that, she shot him a wide smile. "I'll just go and tie Pirate back in the stall and you can go and speak to the Millers. Off you go." She pointed to the house.

To Hannah's surprise, David dutifully headed for the house, leaving her alone sitting on the garden seat.

David had certainly met his match in Mary. Hannah could not resist a chuckle.

By the time Hannah made her way inside, Mary was already in the kitchen helping Mrs. Miller. Hannah heard another buggy arrive outside. "That must be John," Mr. Miller said. "Did you meet him at church today, David?"

It seemed David was back to his old self. A brooding look passed over his face. "*Jah*, only briefly." He shot a look at Hannah under his brows.

Compared to David, John was like a breath of fresh air. He entered the room with a wide smile. "*Denki* for having me to lunch, Mr. Miller," he said.

"Come, take a seat. Lunch is about to begin," Mr. Miller said. "I know this is only a light lunch, because we all had lunch after the meeting and I know you *youngie* want to play volleyball this afternoon. We weren't able to stay for much of the lunch because we had to get home to Esther and Rebecca, who are still not sufficiently recovered to attend the meetings."

Mr. Miller smiled briefly, and then added, "David and John, I believe you two have met?"

John continued to smile widely, but the corners of David's lips curled up ever so slightly. "Yes, we have met," David said in a clipped manner.

Mary came out of the kitchen holding a big tray of baked corn and broke out into a grin when she saw John. "John, remind me to show you Pirate after lunch."

"I've heard quite a bit about this dog."

David tapped his forehead. "I almost forgot. Mary tells me you're looking for a good home for the dog?"

"Yes, we are. Do you want him?" Mrs. Miller said rather too eagerly.

"For all we know the dog has an owner," Mr. Miller began, but David spoke again.

"Yes, I know Pirate might merely be lost, and his owners might come and claim him, but I'd like to look after him until the owners come, and if they never do, then I'd like to keep him."

"You're welcome to him!" Mrs. Miller said enthusiastically. "Can you take him straight after lunch?"

Mary's face fell. Hannah felt sorry for her, but she knew there was no other way.

"Then that's settled then, I suppose," Mr. Miller said somewhat reluctantly.

It occurred to Hannah for the first time that perhaps Mr. Miller might have liked to have a pet, but was unable to do so due to Mrs. Miller's vehement disagreement with the idea. It only strengthened her resolve to have a dog as soon as she was married. *"Nee!"* she said aloud and all eyes turned her.

"What is it?" Esther asked her.

"I just had an unpleasant thought," Hannah said. "*Mamm*, would you like some help?" She only asked her so no one would press her and ask her what the unpleasant thought was. The unpleasant thought, truth be told, was marrying anyone other than Noah Hostetler, but she could scarcely tell that to the others as she could scarcely tell it to herself.

"Are you *ferhoodled*?" Mrs. Miller said. "You know Mary is helping me now, and besides the food is already on the table."

Hannah simply nodded. Still, her mother appeared to be in a better mood, most likely as there were now two suitors for Hannah at the one table. Hannah turned her attention to John and studied him. If Noah had a girlfriend, then Hannah truly would have to move on. There would be no chance of marrying Noah. While she was sure Mrs. Lapp wouldn't have gotten her information wrong, she hoped it was somehow a mistake. Otherwise, if she ever wanted children, she would have to marry someone else. But what if she couldn't ever love another *mann*? Her mother had said that love grows. But what if it didn't?

What if she married someone thinking love would grow and it never did? Would she be satisfied in a loveless marriage if the two of them were friends and she had a lot of *kinner*?

Hannah shook her head. She just couldn't be sure.

"So John, when do you return home?" David asked somewhat enthusiastically.

"In a few days," John said amicably. "The Fischers have invited me to stay for a few more days just to make sure Mary has settled in."

"Oh yes, it's *wunderbar* you're staying a few more days, though I have settled in. Mrs. Miller is lovely and so are Hannah, Esther, and Martha. The *gross-mammi haus* is peaceful and it's nice to have a whole house to myself for the first time in my life. I suppose I'll have to get used to living by myself."

Hannah was shocked. "Why would you say that, Mary? You won't be living by yourself when you get married and have *kinner*."

Mary's face fell. "I don't think I'm ever going to get married."

"Nonsense," Mrs. Miller said firmly. "You'll get married, if I have anything to do with it."

The Miller girls exchanged glances. They had no doubt their mother's words were true. Hannah could see it was like a challenge to Mrs. Miller who couldn't bear to see a girl reach the age of twenty-one without being married. Why, she had as good as told Hannah she was an old maid, and Mary was the same age. Plus Mrs. Miller, despite her exterior, had a kind heart.

"See," John said to his *schweschder*, "you're the only one who thinks you won't get married. Just because the boys at home weren't interested in you, doesn't mean that boys in another community won't be."

David looked up, surprised. "The boys in your community weren't interested in you?" he asked with obvious interest.

Mary, by now, had turned beet red and was staring down at her carrot salad.

Hannah wondered what she could do to rescue the

situation. "So, will your *mudder* mind you taking a dog home?" she asked David.

"*Nee*, my *mudder* is very fond of dogs," he said. "After all, I had a dog for a long time."

Hannah was a little puzzled. "But didn't you say that he died some years ago?"

David nodded. "My mother always wanted to have another dog, but I was too upset after my dog died and couldn't have another. When I saw Pirate, I felt an instant bond with him and I'd really like to have him."

Hannah thought David's words were true. He spoke them earnestly and not with his usual supercilious manner. Perhaps David did have a heart, after all, and didn't people say dogs are good judges of character? Maybe he would be a good husband for some woman after he got over his youthful ways, but certainly she would never entertain the thought of marrying him.

Hannah noticed David shooting a look at John from time to time. "Do you have any plans to come back to this community soon?" David asked John.

David did not appear the least surprised by the question. "Only if Mary asks me to come. Otherwise I'll come to fetch her when she finishes helping the Millers."

"Maybe Mary won't want to leave," Mrs. Miller said. "Maybe Mary will want to stay in this community. Perhaps she will find a husband. In that case, John, you'll have to come and visit Mary, won't you!"

John did look somewhat confused, but simply

said, "*Jah*, I wouldn't like to go too long without seeing my *schweschder*. I'd miss her."

"There are only the two of you, are there?" Mrs. Miller said.

He nodded. "The *doktors* told my mother she would never have *kinner*, but she had the two of us."

"*Kinner* are a blessing from *Gott*," Mrs. Miller said.

Mr. Miller agreed. "Quite so, quite so."

"Will Pirate be all right in your buggy?" Mary asked David.

"I hope so," he said. "All I can do is try to take him a little way and see how he is. If he gets upset, I'll leave him here and come back for him in a taxi."

Hannah had to admit that she was impressed with David's attitude to the dog.

"I do hope Beth doesn't mind you taking him home without telling her first," Mrs. Miller said, frowning. "I hope she doesn't mind," she said again.

"No, she won't mind at all," David reassured her. "And my *schweschder*, Jessie, loves animals too."

Mrs. Miller nodded. "*Jah*, Beth does have several cats." Her hand flew to her mouth. "Cats! I hadn't thought of that. What if the dog chases the cats?"

David also looked concerned. "He's quite a young dog, so hopefully he'll be scared of the cats. I know when *Datt's* friends have visited with their farm dogs, the cats will often spit at them and the dogs are afraid."

"I do hope you're right," Mrs. Miller said.

Hannah knew that Mrs. Miller didn't want to have

to look after Pirate any longer than necessary. Hannah certainly hoped that the dog and the cats would get along.

"I have an idea," Mrs. Miller said. "Why doesn't Hannah ride with you in the buggy to keep the dog happy."

Everyone gasped. "*Nee*," Mr. Miller said. "Rachel, haven you forgotten that Hannah is now afraid of buggies?"

Mrs. Miller sighed. "How silly of me. Forgive me, Hannah. I'd completely forgotten."

That was a lucky escape, Hannah thought. *Thank goodness I'm afraid of buggies now, or sure enough, I would have to ride home with David in the buggy.*

The talk turned from Pirate to the afternoon's volleyball.

"Hannah, Esther, and Martha will be happy when they can go to volleyball again after the meetings," Mr. Miller said. "And Rebecca too, although that will be some time away." His face fell.

Hannah felt a sharp pain of anger against Noah.

"Mary, why don't you go to the volleyball with your *bruder*?" Mrs. Miller said.

Mary looked pleased. "Are you sure? Won't you need help here?"

"Not this afternoon," Mrs. Miller said. "There is only vegetable soup, chow chow and graham cracker pudding for dinner, and you have already helped me prepare that. Besides, you'll be back in time to help me serve dinner, and then you and Hannah can go to the Singing."

"The Singing?" David said sharply. "Hannah, you haven't been to a Singing since the accident."

Hannah simply nodded, but Mrs. Miller said, "Hannah is now recovered sufficiently to go to the Singing. Isn't that right, Hannah?"

Hannah nodded again. She had no desire to go to the Singing, but as it was a place where the *youngie* found potential husbands or wives, her mother was pushing her into it. Sitting for two hours in the one place hurt her leg, which in turn hurt her back. It was entirely uncomfortable and she wasn't looking forward to it. She also didn't want to see Noah with his latest girlfriend.

"What are your Singings like here?" Mary asked Hannah.

It was Mrs. Miller who answered. "Aren't Singings the same everywhere?"

"I don't believe so," Mr. Miller said, "but I do believe our Singing is a fairly typical one, and the *Englischer* visitors we had in the community last month told me so." He chuckled.

"What do you do at your Singings?" Hannah asked Mary.

Mary had a faraway look in her eyes. "We shake the hands of the adults and then we sing. That's about it. Then after we sing for about two hours we eat. There's church spread, corn chips, crackers, popcorn, potato chips, cookies, dessert bars…" Mary paused to scratch her head before continuing. "Of course there's tea and coffee, but my favorite is cocoa. After everyone eats, we leave. My *mudder* says I comfort eat, and I suppose that's true, otherwise I wouldn't have got to this size." She patted her stomach and laughed. John laughed too, as did the girls, but David shot Mary a dirty look.

"Or maybe you'll meet a nice *mann* at the Singing tonight," Mrs. Miller said. "Then you'll want to stay here."

Hannah suspected her mother had taken a liking to Mary, even though she had been there for a short time. She figured her *mudder's* desire to marry Mary to someone in the community was not just her mother's natural desire to marry someone who had reached what her mother considered was the ripe old age of twenty-one, but also because she was fond of the girl and wanted her to stay.

Chapter Fourteen

The large gas heaters the community had brought for the Singing only served to keep the chill off the air, and did nothing to provide any actual warmth unless someone was standing right next to one of them.

Hannah had always enjoyed the Singings before the accident, but tonight was different. Tonight, Noah was there. Of course, he was always at the Singings, but this was the first Singing Hannah had attended after the accident. She fervently wished that Noah was not there.

Why couldn't he have stayed home just this once? she thought. *I just want a little piece of joy in my heart.* Joy was impossible for her now that Noah was there. Her conflicted feelings rose to the surface every time she saw him. *Resentment and love cannot exist in the one heart*, she remembered the bishop saying.

Hannah was concerned. Singings were where boys and girls found someone to date. She had attended Singings since the age of sixteen, like all others in her community. She dreaded seeing Noah with his new girlfriend. No doubt he would drive Susanna home in his buggy.

After the first hour of Singing, Hannah's back was aching. She shifted her weight and wriggled, trying to get feeling back into her legs. A water cup was passed around. It was welcome as Hannah's throat was dry from so much singing. She had grown unaccustomed to it, and wondered if she would lose her voice the following day.

After the first hour of singing slowly, the songs changed to somewhat faster hymns. Hannah would never have known the songs were sung in what was considered by *Englischers* to be an awfully slow manner, if an *Englisch* visitor to the community the previous year hadn't told her.

Several times during the Singing, Hannah felt eyes on her and looked down the row to see David Yoder grinning at her. Each time she smiled politely but briefly and at once looked away. She was glad Mary was with her. Mary had proven she would take no nonsense from David.

After two hours of singing, Hannah had worked up quite a thirst. She looked around for Mary, but she was talking in an animated fashion to a young woman. Hannah walked over to the table that held the food and drink. She looked at the array of cookies and desserts. There were donuts, pies, and cakes. She opted for a glass of water and some coffee. She drank the water in one go and poured herself coffee from the pitcher.

"Can I get anything for you, Hannah?"

Hannah swung around to see Noah's smiling face. *What a silly thing to say*, she thought unkindly. *I'm standing right in front of the food and I could surely get anything I wanted for myself. I don't need him to get me anything.* "I'm fine," she said before she swung around, away from him.

"It was a *gut* Singing, wasn't it?"

Hannah remained with her back to him for a moment, irritated that he would have the nerve even to speak to her. "*Jah*, it was a *gut* Singing." She spoke in as much of a monotone as she possibly could, so as not to discourage him from speaking with her further.

She slowly hobbled away with her *kaffi,* finding a chair away from the group where she could sit by herself. Tonight she just wanted to be left alone. The only reason she had come at all was because her *mudder* had forced her. Her *mudder* was always talking about the time of her youth and what a *gut* time she'd had at all the Singings. She expected Hannah to feel the same way. True, Hannah had always enjoyed the Singings, but she couldn't tonight, not with Noah there.

Noah shrugged and left, and Hannah breathed a sigh of relief. Her relief was short lived, however, for David approached her. "Did you enjoy the Singing, Hannah?"

"*Jah*, it was *gut*." She made to turn away from

David, but he moved closer to her and handed her something.

"Here, try this."

Hannah took the little sugar cake automatically. "*Denki*, David." Hannah did turn away then, but not before she looked up, straight into Noah's eyes. He had clearly been watching the whole exchange. Nee! *Noah will think there's something between me and David, especially given the fact that David stood so close to me*, Hannah thought with alarm. Then she thought about it some more. *So what? What do I care what Noah Hostetler thinks, anyway?*

Hannah studied Noah as he walked over to a group of young people and laughed with them. *It's as if nothing has happened*, she thought. *His life goes on as normal, while he has sent our lives into turmoil.*

Nevertheless, Hannah could not take her eyes off Noah as he made his way around the barn. Her pulse raced faster every time he spoke to another girl. *Surely I can't be jealous*, she thought, as another pang of longing hit her when she took in his tall, muscular frame, his wide shoulders, and his thoughtful, kind face. *I still can't be in love with Noah Hostetler.* Nee, *surely not!*

Hannah put down the plate with the little sugar cake and walked over to the edge of the room to have some privacy. No one else was there due to the fact that it was far from the gas heaters, and so was bitterly cold. Mary was still engaged in conversation with the same young woman.

Hannah looked down at her hands, which felt as

if they were positively freezing. The hand holding her cup of coffee was warming up, but the other one resting on her crutches felt as if it had turned blue.

"Are you cold?"

Hannah looked up to see that Noah had followed her. *"Nee,"* she snapped. She was shocked at her own rudeness, so added, "Well, kind of."

Noah dragged over a bale of hay and sat in front of her.

Why won't he leave me alone? she asked herself silently. *He can surely see that I don't want to speak to him at all.*

"I'm sitting by myself tonight, because I don't feel like company," Hannah said with as much politeness as she could muster. "I don't want to be rude. I'm just saying how it is." She lowered her eyes, hoping he would take her not-so-subtle hint, and then she took a little sip of her *kaffi.*

Noah nodded. "I sometimes feel like that, too. Do you want to know what I do about it?"

Hannah wanted to say, Nee*, I don't care; now go away,* but her *mudder* had brought her up better than that. She took a deep breath. "What do you do about it?"

"I put a smile on my face and all of a sudden the world is brighter."

Hannah could only look at him with irritation. She was sure she had absolutely no expression on her face while she was trying to figure out a way to get him to leave her be.

"Try it now."

Noah was far too cheerful for Hannah. "Try what?"

He clapped both hands onto his knees. "Smile! Try a big smile right now."

"*Nee*, I will not smile. I don't see what there is to smile about. Martha's only just home from the hospital and she's in a lot of pain." She leaned forward and through gritted teeth said, "We've all been through a lot of pain because of..."

"Because of me?" His eyebrows lifted a fraction. "Hannah, I've already said that I'm sorry." He looked intently at Hannah, clearly waiting for a response. When none came, he added, "You know that *Gott* wants us to forgive anyone who asks us."

Hannah could not stop her eyes from rolling. He sounded just like her *daed.*

"I'm truly sorry, Hannah," Noah said. "It was an accident."

Hannah nodded. "*Jah*, I know it was an accident." *But you should have been more careful*, she was longing to say.

Noah rose to his feet. "I guess I'll leave you alone, then." He waited for a moment before he said, "Try that smiling thing once in a while." He walked away without saying another word.

Hannah watched him walk away. She watched him until he joined in with another conversation across the other side of the barn.

Look at him, she thought, *laughing and smiling as if nothing has happened. His life goes on as normal, whereas ours has changed and my parents are forced to take money offerings for the medical bills.* Hannah had to look away from him as bitterness loomed in her heart once again.

Once she had such tender feelings in her heart for Noah, but how could she feel anything for the *mann* who could do something so stupid and then think that just saying *sorry* would fix everything?

Well, sometimes sorry just might not be enough, she thought.

Noah was annoyed with himself. *I can't believe the silly things I said to Hannah,* he scolded himself silently. *Imagine me telling her that* Gott *wants her to forgive me—whatever was I thinking? Nerves just made my mouth run away with me, but that's no excuse for saying such stupid things.* He shook his head. *Hannah will be even more cross with me now. I wish I'd never come to the Singing.*

Noah ran his hands through his hair. *Besides, that David Yoder is clearly keen on Hannah. Hannah doesn't seem interested in him, but what would I know?*

Noah sent up a silent prayer that *Gott* would deliver him out of all of his troubles. He, for sure, could not rely on his own strength to get through them.

Chapter Fifteen

"Hannah! I'm so glad I found you here."

Hannah was sitting on the little wooden seat by the lavender bushes, trying to process her thoughts. "*Hiya*, Mary."

"I was just speaking with Mrs. Miller, and she said I could go and visit Pirate at the Yoders' farm." Hannah opened her mouth to speak, but Mary pushed on. "I miss him so much! I know it's only been a short time, but I really miss having him."

"Do you have a dog at your home?" Hannah asked her.

Mary nodded. "He's my mother's dog. He's like one of the *familye*. My mother wouldn't mind if I had another dog, but we live so far away."

Her face fell and Hannah was concerned that she would start crying. She hurried to reassure her. "I'm sure David is looking after Pirate well."

Mary clapped her hands together. "Well, that's what we're about to find out!"

"We?" Hannah said.

"*Jah*, your mother said you would come with me."

Hannah's hands flew to her throat. "But Mary, I have already told you I'm afraid of buggies." Even the word sent a pang of fear jotting through Hannah's body.

"*Nee, nee.* I have some money of my own and I told your mother I would call a taxi."

Hannah rubbed her forehead. "But Mary, I feel bad that you would have to pay for a taxi simply because I was too afraid to go near a buggy."

"But how else can you come with me?" Mary said. "There's no other way. It's too far to walk, and either I drive the buggy and go alone or we both go in a taxi. Your mother doesn't want me to go alone. Esther and Martha can't come so who else could come with me? If you don't come with me, then I won't be able to visit Pirate."

"In that case, of course I'll come," Hannah said. She could hardly let Mary down, but she certainly did not want to visit David Yoder. She was sure that's why her mother said Mary could visit Pirate.

"Mary, would you mind calling the taxi from the barn and I'll just sit here. You do know the Yoders' address?"

Mary nodded. "Mrs. Miller told me," she said. "*Denki*, Hannah. *Denki* for coming with me."

While Mary was away calling the taxi, Hannah rubbed her eyes. She was glad she wasn't like one of the *Englisch* girls wearing eye make-up, or she would have eyes like a raccoon right now. Hannah chuckled at the thought.

While they waited for the taxi, Mary spoke the whole time in an animated fashion. "I hope Pirate has put on weight! Do you think he's put on weight by now? I know the Yoders haven't had him long, but I hope he's put on weight. You don't think he's been chasing one of their cats, do you?"

Hannah shook her head. "*Nee*, I'm sure *Mamm* would have heard about it by now if he had."

"That such a relief. I liked Pirate immediately, the second I saw him. There's just something about him. Oh, do you think someone has found his owners by now and his owners have come to claim him?"

Hannah shook her head. "No, or *Mamm* would have said," she said wearily.

"That's good!" Mary's face lit up. "I can't wait to see him. You know, Mr. Miller said Pirate was only young, so that means he'll grow a lot more. How tall do you think he'll grow?" Hannah had no chance to answer, because Mary kept talking. "I do hope he's put on some weight. I do hope he's happy living with the Yoders." She seized Hannah's arm. "Oh Hannah, what if he's not happy living with the Yoders? What will we do? I'm sure David won't give him up now."

Hannah sighed. "Let's cross that bridge when we come to it."

The taxi finally arrived, none too soon for Hannah. Mary talked in an animated fashion to the driver all the way to the Yoders' house. Hannah was pleased because it gave her some time to think. She would just have to make sure she stayed close to Mary and away from David. There was no way she would get caught alone with him.

Mary paid the driver, and the taxi drove off. “Where is everyone?” Mary said.

“I suppose we should go to the house,” Hannah said.

They had only taken a few steps toward the house when Pirate appeared. He ran up to Mary and put his paws on her shoulders, nearly knocking her down. She let out a shriek of delight. She flung her hands around Pirate’s neck and showered him with kisses.

David hurried over. “I’m sorry. I’m trying to teach him not to jump up on people.”

“He has put on weight!” Mary shrieked. “He’s fatter. Don’t you think he’s fatter, David?”

“I was hoping he’d put on weight, but it’s hard for me to tell since I see him every day,” David said. “It’s easier for you to tell because it’s been a while since you saw him.”

Mary stopped kissing Pirate’s head and looked up at David. “It seems like you’re taking good care of him.”

David looked somewhat amused. “I am. I told you I would look after him well.”

“So you haven’t heard from his owners yet?”

David shook his head and then shrugged. “The bishop’s made enquiries and no one has come forward. I doubt his owners will ever be found. I wouldn’t be surprised if he was abandoned.”

Mary gasped. "Who would abandon a dog like this? He's not vicious."

"Who would know?" David said. "*Hiya*, Hannah."

"Hullo." Hannah's tone was clipped.

"I hope he hasn't chased your *mudder's* cats," Mary said.

David laughed. "No, he is terrified of them. I don't think he's ever seen a cat before. One of *Mamm's* cats hissed at him and he's been avoiding all of them ever since."

"He's a good dog," Jessie Yoder said walking up behind them. She shot Hannah a dirty look. Hannah wondered what she had done to make Jessie dislike her but as far as she could tell, Jessie was like that with everyone.

Just then, a bird flew past and Pirate ran after it. "Pirate, come back!" David and Mary said in unison. They sprinted after Pirate leaving Hannah alone with Jessie.

"My *bruder's* fond of that dog," Jessie said.

"Yes, he is," Hannah said lamely, not knowing what else to say.

Jessie eyed her speculatively. "Are you still working at Mrs. Hostetler's quilt store?"

Hannah nodded. *"Jah."* She wondered where Jessie was going with this line of questioning.

"Do her sons ever visit?"

"No, not really," Hannah said.

Jessie nodded. "They probably don't have time. I've been in the quilt store from time to time and I've seen Noah, but I'm sure he doesn't have time to go there now he is dating Susana."

Hannah gasped and then caught herself. "He is dating Susana?" She wished she hadn't said something, but then again she really wanted to know.

Jessie looked surprised. "Didn't you know? I thought everyone knew. I hope it wasn't meant to be a secret." She covered her mouth with her hand for a moment. "Please don't tell anyone I told you, or I'll get into even more trouble." With that, she stomped away.

So it was true. Hannah could scarcely believe it. She stood there, numbness overcoming every cell of her body. She barely noticed Mary and David running back with Pirate.

"Hannah, are you all right?" Mary said between gulps of air. "I can hardly speak. Pirate ran so far before we could stop him. I don't think he is a very well-behaved dog, but David is training him."

Mrs. Yoder called out from the house door. "*Hullo*, Hannah. *Hullo*, Mary. Come inside. You too, David."

The three of them walked toward the Yoders' house with Hannah careful to make sure Mary was between her and David. Pirate followed them and then threw himself into a comfortable dog bed next to an Adirondack chair on the porch. Hannah was pleased to see that the dog did indeed seem to be treated as one of the *familye*.

"The dog has settled in well," Mrs. Yoder said. "He's scared of my cats which is just as well for them. It makes it safer all round." She afforded Hannah a small ghost of a smile.

She seems very good with animals, much better than she is with people, Hannah thought.

Mrs. Yoder was still speaking. "There is still a chill to the air so please sit down by the fire and I'll make you all some hot meadow tea."

Hannah walked over to the fire and took off her mittens and warm coat. Mary did likewise. Mary made to sit down and let out a shriek. "There's a cat on the chair! A ginger cat the same color as the wood! Why, I nearly sat on him." She picked up the fat ginger cat and sat down, placing the cat on her knee. He purred so loudly it sounded more like thunder rumbling.

Mrs. Yoder came out with the meadow tea and placed a steaming mug in front of each of them. "You've made a friend there, Mary," she said.

"He's a lovely cat," Mary said. "How many cats do you have, Mrs. Yoder? Are they all inside cats? This one is so warm from sitting by the fire."

Hannah sipped her tea and watched the exchange between Beth Yoder and Mary. Hannah was worried that when Mrs. Yoder and her mother finally realized she would not marry David they might turn their attentions to encouraging Mary to marry David. Beth Yoder had certainly taken a liking to the girl. Maybe it was their shared love of cats.

Mrs. Yoder produced a small black and white cat and showed Mary. "This one was a stray," she told her. "She showed up on my doorstep and she was very thin. We think she was dumped out on the road because she couldn't have long opened her eyes. It took me a long time to get her back to health. She's never grown to her full size."

"Oh, she looks a picture of health now though," Mary said. "Look at her shiny coat and those bright golden eyes."

David crossed the room and sat next to Hannah. "How are you doing, Hannah?" he asked her.

Hannah was dismayed that David was taking advantage of his mother and Mary speaking to each other, thus leaving the two of them alone.

"Gut, denki," Hannah said, not wanting to engage in conversation with David.

"Glad to hear it," he said. "I thought you would be terribly upset that Noah's dating Susanna."

Hannah didn't know what to say, so continued to sip her tea.

"So, are you upset?" David persisted.

Hannah looked up from her tea. "Upset about what?" she asked him.

"Upset about Noah and Susanna dating, of course," David said. "I hope I haven't upset you by mentioning it. You did know, didn't you?"

"Your sister mentioned it earlier," Hannah said.

She hadn't noticed, but Mrs. Yoder had gone to the kitchen and returned with some whoopie pies. She took the plate around and offered the guests and David one in turn. Hannah dutifully selected a chocolate one. She took a large bite, hoping David wouldn't ask her questions while she was eating.

David at last gave up trying to engage her in conversation and was now having a conversation with Mary about the care of cats.

Hannah said back in her seat, relieved. This visit hadn't gone as badly as she thought it would, that was, if it hadn't been for the terrible news about Noah and Susanna.

Chapter Sixteen

Beth Yoder was waiting for Hannah at the door to the little white one-room schoolhouse, her hands firmly planted on her ample hips.

"*Guten mayrie*, Mrs. Yoder."

"Why on earth did you come in that taxi, girl?" That was Mrs. Yoder's only greeting. "It's not far to walk, even with your crutches. The snow is only light. Surely your *daed* would have let you take the buggy?" She shook her head.

Hannah let out a long breath. *This is going to be a difficult morning*, she thought. Aloud she said, "I've been afraid of buggies since the accident, Mrs. Yoder." *And it* is *too far to walk on my crutches*, she added silently.

Beth snorted in disbelief. "What? You find buggies *schecklich*?"

Hannah nodded. "*Jah*, I do, I do find them scary."

Beth snorted again. "I had heard that, but I simply could not believe it. Ask *Gott* to take away your fear. You should give fear no place." Her voice held a clear reprimand.

Easy for you to say, Hannah thought, but just stood there, silent, rubbing her cold hands together. The light snow was rapidly turning to sleet.

Beth was still standing in the doorway. "You have not been in a buggy since the accident?"

"Nee." Hannah hoped that Beth would soon let her inside the schoolhouse where it was surely warmer than outside, and the tiny yet vicious pieces of sleet would not sting her face.

Beth finally moved to let Hannah pass. Hannah shook the snowflakes from her damp hair and hurried inside.

Beth made a sound that sounded like a grunt. "My son, David, could help you overcome your fear. Why don't you come to dinner tonight and he can call for you? He's very good with young horses that are scared of buggies."

Hannah bit her lip. How on earth could she explain an irrational fear to someone? She fought the urge to say, *I'm not a horse*. "*Nee*, Mrs. Yoder, I cannot even get in a buggy. I can't go near one."

To Hannah's relief, Mrs. Yoder merely turned away in obvious disgust. *I hope that's changed her mind about thinking that I'm a suitable* fraa *for her son*, Hannah thought with some amusement.

The day went downhill from there, although it started pleasantly enough with Mrs. Yoder reading the Bible. The children then sang a hymn and recited *The Lord's Prayer*. Hannah had expected she would be able to read to everyone or help in some way, but Mrs. Yoder sharply dismissed her to clean the blackboard. When the blackboard was spotless, despite the fact Mrs. Yoder pointed out some tiny spots that she insisted Hannah had missed, Mrs. Yoder instructed her to bring in firewood.

"I can't, Mrs. Yoder, not with these crutches."

Mrs. Yoder's face was filled with exasperation. "Why did your *mudder* think you would be of help to me then? You're useless!"

Hannah was shocked. She was not usually on the receiving end of such blatant rudeness. "I beg your pardon, Mrs. Yoder," she said in a firm but polite voice, "but I am not useless. It is not my fault that I'm on crutches, and I am doing my best." Hannah said each word slowly in an effort to be more respectful.

Mrs. Yoder's face softened. "Of course it's not your fault—it's that Noah Hostetler's fault. Just sit in that chair over there by the wall, and wait until I think of other duties for you." She rubbed her chin. "Actually, you can poke the fire to keep it going and tidy up those McGuffey Readers. You *can* manage that, can't you?"

Hannah nodded, embarrassed that thirty or so pairs of eyes were upon her and had heard the whole exchange. However, she saw only sympathy on their faces. Mrs. Yoder's forbidding personality had not endeared her to the children. Their usual teacher, Mary Knepp, was a cheerful and pleasant young woman who adored children.

After what seemed like an age, recess arrived.

Hannah looked for somewhere she could take a break in peace, but Beth quickly ushered her over to her seat.

"Come here, we can eat together! I wanted to talk to you about David."

There's a surprise, Hannah thought, but quickly realized that her thoughts were unkind. "David? What about him?"

"I will be forthright. I wanted you to come for dinner as your *mudder* and I would like to see the two of you betrothed. Surely you can see he's a better match for you than that *Noah Hostetler*."

Hannah could not help but notice the malice in Mrs. Yoder's voice when she said Noah's name. In fact, she had almost spat the word. "Oh?" Hannah asked earnestly, "Whatever do you mean?"

"Oh, come now, girl. You can't be with a man like that. You know the sort of thing they get up to when they're with those *Englisch* girls."

Hannah's heart fluttered. *Had Noah been with other girls?* She couldn't help but worry.

"I, I don't know. Do you really think Noah is the sort of man to do that?" she stammered.

Mrs. Yoder was all too quick to reply. "Of course he is. You can't think a *mann* that reckless as to cause your accident wouldn't jump at the chance to be with an *Englisch* girl, surely." Beth leaned in closer. "I don't mean to sound mean-spirited, but I think he may be of a bad sort."

Hannah knew Beth was trying to make Noah seem like a bad person, but she couldn't help but let it upset her. *Is Noah a bad person?* She looked down to her leg and at her crutches. Had Noah been with *Englisch* girls, or other girls at all? Her stomach twisted into a knot.

Hannah, of course, realized what was happening: Beth was trying hard to turn her away from Noah, so that she would look favorably upon David—but she was not in love with David, and never would be. Yet the saying *"Wu Schmook iss, iss aa Feier," Where there's smoke, there's fire*, kept running through her mind, and try as she might, she could not get it to go away.

Hannah longed to ask Mrs. Yoder to clarify. She longed to ask, "Do you actually know that Noah has been seeing a girl?" but she did not want to give her the satisfaction. Also, Mrs. Yoder had implied that Noah was running around with *Englisch* girls, but had not said so outright.

Suddenly, Hannah had a moment of clarity. What if Noah actually *was* with another girl? It would be none of Hannah's business. They were not engaged to be married; they were not even dating. Noah was perfectly well within his rights to date another girl. Tears pricked at Hannah's eyes. Why did she care so much?

At the end of the school day, Hannah discovered that Mrs. Yoder had assumed that she was, in fact, accompanying her home for dinner, and that Hannah's *mudder* was aware of this. Hannah groaned inwardly.

Mrs. Yoder expected Hannah to walk with her to her *haus*. It was not far away for someone who was able-bodied, but Hannah found it difficult on her crutches. The snow and sleet had stopped, which made the journey easier than it otherwise might have been, but Mrs. Yoder waited impatiently for Hannah every few yards.

Once inside the house, Hannah made to help Mrs. Yoder in the kitchen, but she shooed her away. "Go sit on the porch, Hannah. David will be here soon, and you two young folks can talk. I'll bring you some hot tea to warm you up."

Could she be any more obvious? Hannah thought.

Hannah sat alone on the porch, shivering in the late winter air, until Mrs. Yoder returned with a steaming mug of hot tea.

"*Denki*, Mrs. Yoder." Hannah wrapped her cold hands around the mug.

"I hope one day you will call me *Mamm*." Mrs. Yoder winked at Hannah and then left.

Hannah sat with her mouth open. *I suppose I should be grateful that Mrs. Yoder is so surprisingly frank. At least there are no undercurrents of deception*, she thought. *She has me all but married to David already*. Hannah gave an involuntary shudder at the thought. *I'd rather be an old maid than married to David!*

"Cold?"

Hannah looked up to see David standing in front of her. She had been too lost in thought to notice his approach, and hadn't even noticed Pirate. David's younger *schweschder*, Jessie, hurried past him into the house. Clearly Jessie had been dispatched by Mrs. Yoder to fetch David in from work on the farm.

"*Hullo*, David. *Jah*, I'm a little cold. Can we go back inside the *haus*?"

A momentary look of annoyance flashed across David's face. Hannah figured that he had recognized her attempt to avoid being alone with him. Maybe she hadn't been that subtle, after all.

"*Nee*, you will soon warm up with the hot tea—and the *gut* company," he added, with what he no doubt thought was a charming smile.

Hannah replied by way of a stiff smile. She didn't wish to be rude or unpleasant to the Yoders, but they were not making it easy. It should be plain to them that she had no interest in David, but neither David nor his *mudder*, Beth Yoder, seemed to be taking the hint. How could she hold David at arms' length and remain polite? The only solution she could see was to be dating another *mann*, but the only *mann* she had ever had feelings for was Noah. And Hannah was a very long way from sorting out those feelings.

After an awkward time of stilted conversation, Jessie came to fetch Hannah and David inside for dinner. David put his hand around Hannah's arm to help her to her feet, and it was all she could do not to pull away. She stepped over Pirate who had fallen asleep and was snoring softly.

Mr. Yoder arrived moments later. He nodded to Hannah. Hannah knew him as a quiet *mann* who never had much to say, but he seemed kindly enough. Hannah had been to the Yoders many times before when it was their turn to have church in their *haus*, but never had she been to their *haus* by herself. She felt most uncomfortable.

"Let us pray."

Hannah glanced up at Mr. Yoder and then bowed her head for the silent prayer before dinner. She did her best not to squirm in her chair, which was the hardest chair she had ever encountered, and her hip was aching from having had to walk so far and from sitting for two hours on a hard seat at the Singing the previous night. Even the normally pleasant aroma of chicken pot pie did not help, but merely served to make her feel slightly nauseous.

There was at first no talk during the meal, and Hannah was in two minds about how she felt about that. On the one hand, she was grateful not to have to make conversation, but the other hand, it was so quiet that one could hear a pin drop, and Hannah felt as if everyone could hear her chewing loudly. Her nerves were on edge. The clock chimed again, as it did every quarter hour, and Hannah jumped.

Hannah was the last to finish her food and felt as though all eyes were on her. She hurried to eat the last of the mashed potatoes covered with gravy on her plate. When Mrs. Yoder and Jessie stood up to clear away the plates, Hannah struggled to her feet to help.

"*Nee*, Hannah, you stay here at the table. *Denki* for offering, though; you will make *someone* a *gut* wife." To Hannah's horror, Mrs. Yoder winked at David when she said it.

They think it's a done deal, Hannah thought with considerable dismay. *What am I going to do?* Hannah figured that the one small relief was that the lights in the room were dim, so no one would see her horrified expression. Hannah's family had propane-powered lights, whereas the Yoders had kerosene lights, and those gave off far less light.

Mrs. Yoder and Jessie soon returned to the table and deposited plates with heaped servings of Cinnamon Chip Bread Pudding. "This is David's favorite," Mrs. Yoder said pointedly, looking at Hannah. "He especially likes the warm vanilla milk topping. One day I'll show you how to make it just how David likes it."

Hannah fought the sudden urge to run out the door. She was worried an anxiety attack was coming on, although those had only previously threatened when she was faced with a buggy or going to the hospital.

To Hannah's surprise, the usually sullen Jessie spoke up. "*Mamm,* Hannah mightn't want to marry David. People should marry whoever they like, even if their parents don't approve."

Mrs. Yoder gasped aloud at her *dochder's* rudeness, and Mr. Yoder snapped a sharp, "Jessie, apologize!"

"Sorry, *Mamm, Datt.*" Her voice was meek, but not believably so.

Hannah shot Jessie a quick smile, but Jessie merely glowered at her from under her eyelashes.

What was that about? Hannah wondered. *I*

thought she was trying to help me, but she must have her own agenda.

At least Jessie's outburst seemed to have set everyone to talking.

"How's your leg now, Hannah?" David asked. "Will you be off crutches soon?"

"Jah, denki," Hannah said, avoiding looking directly at David. "The *doktor* said it's not healing as fast as he'd like, but even so, he said I won't need crutches much longer."

"That Noah Hostetler should be ashamed," Mrs. Yoder spat, but was brought up short by her husband.

"*Ach!* There'll be no such talk here. We must all forgive one another as Christ forgave us." Mr. Yoder's voice was calm but authoritative.

Mrs. Yoder looked as if she were about to say something further, but Jessie butted in first. "It's not Jacob's fault that Noah caused the accident. You can't help who your *bruder* is. Oh, no offense, David."

David merely chuckled, but a nasty, red flush traveled up Mrs. Yoder's face.

"There will be no more talk of Jacob Hostetler," she said, glancing sideways at her husband. "And I will speak to you later, *dochder*."

Jessie's face grew even more sullen and she narrowed her eyes.

Hannah watched the exchange with interest. *So that's what it's all about*, she thought. *Jessie's sweet on Jacob Hostetler. I wonder if Esther knows? I've known for a while that Esther feels the same way about Jacob. I hope Jessie doesn't prove to be a rival for Jacob's affections.*

Hannah wondered how early she could leave the Yoders' *haus* and remain within the bounds of good manners. After the table was cleared, Hannah cleared her throat. "*Denki* so much for having me, Mr. and Mrs. Yoder, but I must be getting home. *Mamm* needs my help with Esther and Martha."

Mrs. Yoder looked most affronted. "Nonsense, child, your *mudder* told me she can manage with your *schweschders* tonight now that she has Mary's help. She said you needed a well-earned rest."

Hannah was panic-stricken at the thought of having to spend any longer in the uncomfortable presence of the Yoders. She suspected that Mrs. Yoder would soon maneuver her into being alone with David again. "*Nee*, *denki*, but I must go."

A calculating look passed across Mrs. Yoder's face. "Okay then. David, go with Hannah to the barn so she can call for a taxi."

Hannah thought for a moment. She could hardly refuse to go with David to the barn. She considered asking if David could go by himself, but clearly, Mrs. Yoder's patience had already worn thin. She simply said, "*Denki*, Mrs. Yoder."

David opened the door for Hannah. She pulled up short when a blast of cold air hit her in the face. "My, it's cold for this time of year! You'd think it was the middle of winter rather the end of winter."

David simply smiled at her and tried to take her arm again.

Hannah sidestepped to avoid him. "*Nee*, David, *denki*. I can manage."

Pirate ran inside, past both of them. He soon turned tail and ran back outside. Hannah assumed he had seen one of the cats. He returned to his dog bed and promptly fell asleep.

David stepped into the darkness with a lamp. Hannah hobbled out to the barn after David, hoping that the taxi would come quickly. Once inside the relative warmth of the barn, David showed her where the phone was, and held up the lamp for her.

Hannah made the call and then turned to David. "Let's get back to the *haus* where it's warm." She rubbed her hands together to emphasize that she was cold.

David put the lamp on the ground and stood in front of her. "Why the hurry?" The lamplight flickered across the angles of his face, making him appear menacing.

A chill ran up Hannah's spine. "I want to go to the *haus*, David, *now*," she said, in the firmest tone she could muster. She hoped her voice wasn't shaking as much as she was on the inside.

David took a step closer to her. "How about a little kiss before you go?"

Hannah caught her breath. "*Nee*, David!"

David moved so close there was barely anything between them. "Oh come on, *schatzi*! You know you want to kiss me."

"I am *not* your sweetheart and I do *not* want to

kiss you. Now let me pass or I will call for your *mudder*!"

Hannah's threat seemed to have no effect on David. He took Hannah by the shoulders and pulled her to him, his lips reaching for hers.

Hannah told hold of both of her crutches, and jabbed them down hard on the top of his foot. David released her with a yelp of pain.

Hannah hobbled off to the *haus* as fast as she could. In fact, she reached the *haus* before David did.

Mrs. Yoder met her at the door. "Where's David?"

"He's right behind me." Hannah pushed past Mrs. Yoder and hurried into the *haus* before Mrs. Yoder could tell her to wait with David on the porch for the taxi. As far as Hannah was concerned, that had been the last *alone time* she was ever going to spend with David Yoder.

Chapter Seventeen

Hannah had considerable trouble falling asleep that night. After she had arrived home, her *mudder* had questioned her about the night, but Hannah had told her firmly yet politely that she was not interested in David Yoder and never would be, even if he were the last *mann* on earth. Her *mudder* had looked surprised. Whether it was due to Hannah's vehement tone or her actual words, Hannah did not know, but she was grateful that her *mudder* had not said much at all in reply.

As Mary was already gone home to the *gross-mammi haus* for the night, Hannah made sure Esther and Martha were settled, and refilled their hot water bottles, which had gone cold. She snuggled under her quilt, but sleep eluded her. Her whole day had been unpleasant, but the incident with David had upset her. If only she were betrothed to another *mann*, and then David would leave her alone.

Noah would make sure that David didn't bother

me, she thought, and then she at once reprimanded herself for thinking such a thing. Besides, Mrs. Yoder had said that Noah had been seen with *Englisch* girls. While Mrs. Yoder clearly wanted to turn Hannah away from Noah, that didn't mean that she wasn't telling the truth.

When the sun forced its way through the dark clouds at dawn, Hannah was still awake. She wasn't sure whether she had slept from time to time in short spurts, but it seemed to her that she'd been awake all night. Her leg ached and her back hurt, and she felt as though she were coming down with a cold.

Hannah was looking forward to working at Katie Hostetler's store that day because she could have a nice rest. She was due for a doctor's appointment and was worried he would lecture her for not resting up. She was rested more now Mary had arrived on the scene, but she was certain she had not rested enough to suit the doctor.

Katie took one look at her and ushered her into the back room. "Hannah, is something the matter? Here, I'll make you some *kaffi*."

Hannah sighed. "I've been sitting a lot lately. The Singing was the first one I had been to in a while, and sitting for so long hurt my back and my legs."

A flash of concern passed over Katie's face. "Will you be all right to sit today for a few hours?"

Hannah nodded. "Of course." Even as she said it, she wasn't so sure her words were true. "At least the seat in the store is nicely padded," she said more to reassure herself than Katie.

Katie nodded. "That's *gut.* Well, it's a busy day today. Some more orders came in at the end of last week. Have you been getting enough sleep, Hannah?"

"Probably not," Hannah said truthfully, and was grateful when Katie didn't ask her why. Perhaps she already suspected, but that thought made Hannah uncomfortable.

Hannah did feel marginally better after drinking some *kaffi*, even though she'd had two cups of strong *kaffi* at home that day and had even finally given in and tried some of Mary's *kaffi oats*, which was nowhere near as bad as it sounded. In fact, Hannah thought she might develop a taste for it. She chuckled to herself.

The day had started overcast, but now the sun was peeping through the clouds on occasion. It looked like the promised storm would come to nothing, so with the brightening of the sun came the brightening of Hannah's mood. The chair was well-padded and comfortable and supported Hannah's back in the right places, so soon Hannah felt her whole body relax.

She looked up when the first customer for the day entered the shop. To her shock, it was Susanna, Noah's new girlfriend, at least, according to Mrs. Lapp.

Katie greeted her warmly. "*Hiya*, Susanna. What can I do for you today?"

"I want to buy some fabric for a new quilt I'm making."

"What type of quilt have you decided to make?" Katie asked her.

Susanna tapped her chin. "I actually haven't quite decided yet. Maybe a Log Cabin, or a Broken Star. I'm not very good at deciding. Do you have any suggestions?"

"Well, of course, it's up to you," Katie said. "What type of quilt would you like to make? Are you making it for yourself, or for a gift?"

"I thought of making it for myself, but I don't really know what to make. I thought of the Log Cabin, but I also thought of the Star of Bethlehem, or the Dresden Platc. I also likc the Tree of Life." She broke off and gave a nervous giggle. "I also thought I might like to make a Double Wedding Ring quilt."

"Oh, do you have a young *mann* in mind?" Katie asked her.

"Jah," Susanna said with a nervous giggle, putting both her palms over her eyes.

Hannah was surprised. Didn't Katie know about Susanna and her son, Noah? Why, Mrs. Lapp had told her Noah was dating someone, but then again, she had seemed surprised. Surely Katie would have gone straight home and asked Noah if he was dating a girl. Hannah would be surprised if Noah denied such a thing.

Hannah thought on it some more, and then wondered if Katie was acting as if she didn't know Noah and Susanna were dating to spare her. Yes, that must be it. Hannah nodded slowly to herself.

Susanna hunched over some quilting-weight fabric for a while and then looked up at Katie. Hannah was doing her best not to stare, but could hardly help overhearing the conversation, so small was the store.

"*Jah*, I've decided. I would like to make a Double Wedding Ring quilt."

"That's a good idea," Katie said. "Every girl of your age should make a Double Wedding Ring quilt. Are you looking to buy some of the fabric today?"

Susanna nodded. "I've just finished making a Starburst quilt, and before that I made a Loan Star quilt, so I think it's time."

The women stopped talking while Katie showed Susanna various fabrics. It took Susanna an inordinately long time to decide. Hannah wondered what was taking her so long and figured there must be something on her mind.

Finally, Susanna said, "Mrs. Hostetler, does your *familye* ever visit you here?"

Katie appeared surprised by the question. "*Nee*, not really. I have no *dochders*, and of course my sons have no interest in my store. They have no occasion to come here."

Susanna's face fell. "Oh, was at the café across the road last week and I thought I saw Noah come in here. It was at this time of day."

Katie darted a quick look at Hannah, who looked away at once. "*Jah*, but that was unusual. He rarely comes here. What you ask?"

Hannah looked up again to see Susanna's face flush beet red. "Oh no reason, really," she said.

After an interval where the two of them stood

around awkwardly, or so it seemed to Hannah, Susanna said, "I spoke to Noah at the Singing."

"Jah," was all Katie said. "All my sons went to the Singing. Did you speak to my other sons, too?"

"*Nee*, only to Noah." Susanna appeared to be searching Katie's face.

Hannah wondered what all that was about. Surely then, Noah hadn't driven Susanna home in his buggy. Hannah's heart leaped at the thought, but then she realized Katie wouldn't know whether or not Noah—of course he would have driven home alone and she would have no idea what time he was due home. That is, of course, unless all the Hostetler *bruders* had gone in the one buggy, but Hannah had no way of knowing if that was the case. And why was Susanna so keen to bring up Noah's name to Mrs. Hostetler?

Hannah thought on it some more and then finally decided she had the answer. Maybe Noah didn't want his mother to know he was dating Susanna, so Susanna was mentioning him to Katie to try to gauge her reaction in some way.

Hannah shook her head. No, that didn't quite make sense. The whole matter was confusing. It was clear to her that Susanna was keen on Noah; that was for sure and for certain.

After Susanna paid for the fabric, she walked over to Hannah. "*Hiya*, Hannah."

Hannah returned the greeting. *"Hullo."*

"I saw you at the Singing. It's *gut* that you're well enough to go to the Singings again."

Hannah nodded. *"Jah,"* she said, feeling quite awkward.

"I saw Noah speak to you at the Singing."

Hannah did not know how to respond so simply said *"Jah"* again.

Susanna searched her face, and then asked, "How long have you been working here?"

"Not long," Hannah said shifting in her seat. She was decidedly uncomfortable. Fortunately, Katie came to her rescue.

"Is there anything else I can show you, Susanna?"

Susanna looked around the store. "There was something else I wanted, but I can't remember what it is now."

"Well, you can return when you think of it," Katie said.

Susanna nodded and left the shop. Katie walked back to speak to Hannah, but just then, an *Englisch* customer entered the store.

Hannah wondered what all that was about. Was Susanna jealous of her speaking with Noah at the Singing? It certainly seemed that she was. Yet if Susanna was, in fact, dating Noah, she would have no reason to be jealous. Hannah thought some more. Maybe the fact that Susanna was dating Noah was the reason she was jealous.

Hannah stopped sewing and put her head between her hands. This was all too much.

After the *Englisch* customer left, Katie walked back over to Hannah. "Hannah, you're looking pale. I want you to leave a little early today."

Hannah protested. “I must stay and work here.”

Katie looked at her for a moment. “I want you to leave half an hour early, but I’ll still pay you for that time.” Hannah made to protest, but Katie held up her hand, palm outward. “*Nee*, I insist. I want you to go to that little café down the road and sit there and have *kaffi* and cake.” She pulled something out of her apron and put it in front of Hannah. “Here’s a coupon for *kaffi* and cake of your choice. I’m friends with the owner and she often gives me coupons. Now, I don’t want you to argue because it will make me feel better. You haven’t been yourself all day and I’m worried about you. I would worry about you all afternoon if you didn’t take this well-earned break for yourself.”

Hannah thought about arguing some more, but then thought it would do no good. “*Denki*, Katie,” was all she said by way of response.

It wasn’t that Hannah was physically sick; it was that the exchange with Susanna had left her somewhat noxious. Her stomach was churning. Yes, alone time was exactly what she needed. She would find a place to sit at the back of the café and relax.

Hannah was relieved Katie had let her go early. She had intended to sit in a café by herself for a short time until her doctor’s appointment, but this would give her longer. She wanted time to herself to collect her thoughts.

As Hannah walked into the café that was down the road from the quilt store and where she had been many times before, she saw to her dismay it was crowded. She walked a little ways into the café, but all the seats were taken.

Hannah walked back out. She knew there was another café nearby, but it seemed her cast got heavier and heavier by the day. She certainly hoped the doctor would tell her she could have it off, especially after the X-ray she'd had the previous week. Still, the X-ray technician had warned her that the doctor might put her in a splint. She certainly hoped that was not the case. Hannah just wanted to be able to walk again normally and not hop everywhere. She realized how she had taken little things for granted and made a promise to herself she would never take anything for granted again.

When she reached the other café, it seemed just as crowded, but on closer inspection there were spare tables. At least she had a coupon for this café. She walked through the glass doors and made her way into the back section. Hannah was dissatisfied to see that all those tables were full, so she turned around and finally sat at a table for two near the entrance. It afforded a good view of the street, but it also afforded passersby a good view of her. Hannah shook her head to dismiss such thoughts. What did it matter if people looked in the window at her? *It doesn't matter at all,* she told herself silently.

She was wondering if there was table service when a waitress appeared at the table. "I have a coupon for coffee and cake," she said, showing the waitress. "What sort of coffee and cake can I have?"

"Any you like, even a large sized coffee," the waitress told her, "and you can select any of the cakes in the display cabinet over there." She nodded in the direction behind Hannah.

"Could you suggest one?" Hannah asked her. "I have a cast on my leg and I'd rather not have to get up again."

"Of course. Now let me see, we have chocolate mud cake, carrot cake, raspberry cheesecake, marble cake, blueberry muffins, triple chocolate muffins, sticky buns…" The waitress's voice trailed away and she peered behind Hannah at the selection of cakes.

"Raspberry cheesecake sounds good, please," Hannah said, "and some black coffee. Do I give my coupon to you now or when I leave?"

The waitress smiled at her. "Just give it to me now. That will be fine."

Hannah idly looked out the window at the passers-by while waiting for her food to arrive. She was agitated, and figured that she was apprehensive about the doctor's appointment.

"Hannah," came a masculine voice behind her.

Her heart constricted for a moment, thinking it was Noah's voice, but she realized it wasn't. She partly swung around to see John. "*Hiya*, John. What are you doing here?"

"Quite the same thing as you are, I expect," he said with a laugh. "I'm here to eat. I was exploring town before I go back home in a few days."

Hannah noticed he was looking at her expectantly so she said, "Would you like to join me?"

He took a seat opposite her, and said, "Do they have good coffee here?"

Hannah shrugged one shoulder. "I have no idea. I used to go to the café a block from here, but they were too full." After she said that she wondered if John had seen her through the window and had come in for that reason.

The waitress came over to take John's order. He ordered a large lunch of fried chicken and waffles as well as French toast with maple whipped cream. When the waitress left, he said, "Mary tells me you work at a quilt store every morning."

"Not every morning," Hannah corrected him. "I work three days a week for Mrs. Hostetler."

He scratched his head. "Hostetler. Oh yes, I met the Hostetler *bruders* on Sunday. There are five of them, aren't there?"

"Four," Hannah said.

"Oh I see," he said. "I have enjoyed being in your community, Hannah."

Hannah simply nodded. She hoped John wasn't attracted to her because she was not attracted to him. However, he seemed nice.

"I enjoyed dinner at your house the other night," he continued.

"Denki," Hannah said automatically.

"Mary enjoys helping your mother," he said. "She enjoys living by herself in the *grossmammi haus* too. I think she finds helping your *mudder* far more enjoyable than doing farm work." He chuckled. "I think I've said 'enjoy' about five times in a row."

"Oh yes, *Mamm* enjoys having Mary around too," Hannah said. She laughed as well. "Now I've said it."

John joined in the laughter. "Mary sure was attached to that dog," he said after an interval.

"Pirate," Hannah supplied. "Yes, I'm sure she dearly wanted to keep him, but *Mamm* is very much opposed to having pets."

John nodded. "*Jah*, Mary told me that herself. I think she was hoping I could take the dog home with me but it just wouldn't be possible. Still, it seems like he has gone to a good home."

"Yes, he has. David Yoder said Mary was welcome to visit Pirate at any time. I'm sure she'll continue to do that."

"Yes, it was kind of you to take her," John said. "Do you mind me asking why you are afraid of buggies?"

Hannah looked at him. "Since my accident, I'm afraid of buggies. I can't even go in one."

"If you don't mind me asking, are you and David Yoder dating?"

"Nee," Hannah said forcefully and probably a little too loudly. She felt her cheeks burn. "No, I'm not," she amended in a softer voice. When she looked back at John, he seemed pleased.

John opened his mouth to say something, but Hannah was afraid he would ask her on a buggy ride, so she quickly said, "I'm seeing the doctor this afternoon to see if I can have my cast taken off. I certainly hope I can because it's so difficult walking around in this heavy cast and I take so long to get anywhere on my crutches."

John appeared embarrassed, so Hannah thought she might have been correct in thinking he would ask her on the buggy ride. "Oh," was all he said.

"Yes, and the X-ray technician told me I might have to go into a split," Hannah said. "I certainly hope not." It was then she realized she had only just told John she was afraid of buggies, so he would hardly ask her on a buggy ride. Still, that didn't mean he wouldn't ask her on some other type of date. "You must be happy to go home. You must be missing everyone," Hannah said, and then wished she hadn't said such a thing because John might think she was trying to find out whether he had a girlfriend.

It appears her worst fears were right. "There's no one special waiting for me," he said in a warm tone.

Hannah bit her lip. The waitress placed a steaming mug of coffee and a plate with a large slice of strawberry cheesecake in front of her. If Hannah hadn't been so hungry she would have considered leaving right then and there.

"Please go ahead and don't wait for me," David said. "You don't want to be late for your appointment."

"Denki," Hannah said, grateful that eating would give her excuse not to speak further to John. He seemed a lovely person. He just wasn't for her. She wondered if there was some way she could give Mary the hint that she wasn't interested so she could pass it onto her *bruder*.

John did not speak again and Hannah was quite uncomfortable eating with him sitting there. She had so wanted time by herself to think things over. This had certainly gone against her plans.

Finally, John's food arrived. "Thank goodness," he said fervently. "I'm starving, not that you'd think so to look at me." He patted his stomach and pulled a funny face.

Hannah could not resist laughing, and John laughed too. At that moment, she looked out the window and saw Noah looking at her. She paused, her spoon halfway to her lips. Noah did not look pleased. She could see how it looked—it looked as though she were engaged in a happy animated conversation with John and maybe even looked as though they were dating.

Then again, why should she care what Noah Hostetler thought of her?

Noah stood rooted to the spot. There was his beloved Hannah laughing with John Beiler. Could Jessie Yoder be right? Were Hannah and John actually dating? He didn't think it true when Jessie had told him on Sunday, but there was the evidence right front of his eyes. Besides, Hannah wasn't at the café right next to his mother's store, so was she trying to hide?

Noah realized he was staring, so forced himself to walk on further.

He was sick to the stomach.

Chapter Eighteen

When the taxi arrived at the doctor's office, Mrs. Miller was already waiting for Hannah outside. Hannah paid the driver but struggled to get out of the car.

"Am I late, *Mamm*?" she asked her *mudder*.

"*Nee*, I think I'm a little early."

"I hope this cast can come off today," Hannah said with a sigh.

"Of course it will," Mrs. Miller said. "You have been taking comfrey according to Mrs. Graber's instructions and I'm sure that has helped your bones knit together well."

Hannah nodded. She didn't want to get her hopes up. "I hope I don't have to wear a splint," she said.

"Why are you in such a mood today, Hannah? Has something happened?"

Hannah leaned on her crutches and waved one hand. "I think I'm just apprehensive about this appointment."

Her mother simply shot her a look as the automatic doors opened for both of them to walk in. The waiting room was fairly empty, and the receptionist informed them that the doctor was running late.

"Doctors are always running late," Mrs. Miller said to Hannah as an aside. She indicated they should sit on the red plastic chairs at the far end of the room. "Have you given any more thought to what I said to you?" she asked.

Hannah was genuinely puzzled. "About what?"

Mrs. Miller frowned deeply. "About getting married, of course. Hannah, I know you think you have all the time in the world, but those years pass by in a flash. I keep telling you this. Soon you'll be old and alone and with no *kinner*. Is that what you want? I've said this before and I'll say it again. Do you want to see your *schweschders* all married and all with their own *kinner* while you're living alone in a *grossmammi haus* and while your *schweschders* even have grandchildren? Is that what you want?"

"No..." Hannah began, but her mother interrupted her.

"Hannah, it's no use having your head in the clouds any longer. This is reality. Unless a new *mann* comes in from another community, then you will have to marry someone you already know. So who is it to be?"

Hannah gasped. "*Mamm*, I just can't marry someone I don't love."

Mrs. Miller's face grew redder. Hannah was glad there were no pots and pans for her to bang around. "You have choices. Most girls don't have choices, but you do. There is David Yoder and there's John Beiler. I've seen the way both of them look at you and I am sure you could marry either of them. So who do you choose?"

"It isn't that simple," Hannah said in desperation.

Her mother shook her head. "To the contrary, it *is* that simple. Don't let this opportunity pass you by. When you look back and regret not getting married, it will all be too late. You will be an old maid and no one will want you. Is that what you want?"

Hannah shook her head.

"I know you think I'm being hard on you and perhaps you even think I'm being unreasonable, but I do have your best interests at heart. You're already older than you should be to get married. I was eighteen when I married your father. Hannah, you can't let this keep dragging on thinking something is going to change. Things won't change unless you make them change."

Thankfully for Hannah, the doctor summoned her into the room. At least she had forgotten all her apprehension about the appointment due to her mother insisting that she marry either David or John. She shuddered at the thought.

The doctor spent some time looking at papers on his desk and then looked up. "The X-rays you had last week look promising."

"Does that mean the cast can come off?" Hannah said in delight.

He afforded her a brief smile. "Yes."

"Do I need to wear a splint?" Her stomach clenched at the thought.

"No, you don't, but I must caution you to continue to rest."

Continue to rest? Hannah thought. *I haven't really rested at all. Not unless you count working at Mrs. Hostetler's.*

The doctor was still speaking. "I'll schedule another X-ray in a month just to make sure your leg is progressing nicely. But please don't think you can go back to normal with your leg right away. You still need to give it special care so that the bones can continue to heal."

Hannah nodded.

He stood up and picked up a scary looking instrument. "This is a special saw for taking off the cast," he said. "You'll feel a vibration, but it won't hurt."

As he removed the cast, Hannah fought the desire to laugh. She didn't know if it was from the fact that the cast tickled as it came away or whether it was hysterical laughter from her mother trying to pressure her to marry.

As soon as the cast was off, Hannah made to rub her leg. The doctor waved a finger at her. "Whatever you do, don't rub your leg or scratch it. It's going to be itchy and the skin will be sensitive for a while. I suggest rubbing lotion onto it but be very gentle with it."

"Thank you, doctor," Hannah said. She looked with dismay at her leg. The skin was pale, flaky, and dry.

"And wash it in mild soap and water," the doctor continued. "Make sure you are gentle with it. And like I said, continue to rest up. You don't want to go back into a cast now, do you?"

"No, I don't," Hannah said with feeling.

"Try on your shoe. Did you bring a boot in a bigger size as I suggested?"

Hannah produced two boots from the bag her mother had given her, and handed them to the doctor. "I have my father's old boot which I think will be too big, and one of my own boots."

The doctor looked at both boots. "Your leg isn't as swollen as I thought it might be. Try on your own boot and see how it feels."

Hannah tentatively wedged the boot onto her foot. It felt strange, but Hannah figured that was simply because her leg had been in a cast for so long. "It doesn't feel tight," she told the doctor.

The doctor cautioned her about blisters and then dismissed her.

Mrs. Miller looked up as Hannah walked out of the doctor's office rather unsteadily. Hannah was dizzy, and it was strange to walk without a cast when she had worn one for so long. Mrs. Miller stood up, a wide smile on her face. "*Wunderbar!* The cast is off. I take it you don't need a splint?"

"Nee," Hannah said. "I feel quite strange though, walking."

"That's to be expected," her mother said. "What did the *doktor* say?"

"He said I have to rest up and he has scheduled another X-ray for next month," Hannah told her. "The bone still has healing work to do."

Her mother nodded. "Let's go home. Will you go by taxi, or will you come with me in the buggy?"

When Hannah looked horrified, her mother added, "Oh, I'm sorry. I didn't realize you would still be scared of buggies."

"It wasn't because of the cast that I was scared of buggies," Hannah said, frowning. She wondered why her *mudder* would think such a thing. Did she think the cast was the last reminder of the accident, so Hannah would suddenly have no mental scars?

"*Nee*, of course not. All right then, I have shopping to do so I will see you at home. Your *vadder* and your *schweschders* will be pleased that your cast has been removed. And I will visit Rebecca this afternoon," Mrs. Miller said. "You need to rest your leg since it's newly out of its cast."

Hannah knew there would be no use arguing with her mother when she had her mind made up.

When Hannah arrived home, Esther and Martha let out a squeal of delight. "Your cast has gone!" they said in unison.

Hannah laughed. "My leg feels strange," she told them, "but I'm so pleased the cast is off."

Mary came out of the kitchen, wiping her hands on a towel. "Hannah, that's *wunderbar.* You must be so pleased. Does it feel funny?"

"Yes, it does," Hannah admitted. "I feel I'm all out of balance like I'm tilting to one side. After all, I've had the cast on for a few weeks now."

"Rebecca will be out of the hospital soon and our backs are getting better," Esther said. "Soon we will all be as good as new."

Hannah didn't think she'd ever be as good as new, but simply smiled at her sister. "I'll make everyone some meadow tea," Mary said as she scurried back to the kitchen.

Martha went back in to lie on her mattress and read a book. Hannah walked over to Esther who spoke to her in lowered tones. "Are you all right? You look worried. Is it just that you feel strange having your cast off?"

"It's *Mamm*. She gave me a strict talk today about getting married soon," Hannah confessed.

"Who to exactly?" Esther asked.

Hannah almost laughed at the horrified look on Esther's face. "She said David or John." Hannah cast a glance toward the kitchen as she said John's name. She certainly didn't want Mary overhearing.

"Well, John seems nice," Esther said.

"Yes, he is, but I'm not in love with him."

Esther nodded. "Of course not. Hannah, what about Noah?"

"Noah?" Hannah said loudly, and Martha turned to look at her. Lowering her voice, she added, "Why would you say such a thing?"

"Because you were always in love with him," Esther pointed out.

Hannah had no words. She just shook her head. "I can't," she finally said. After a few more moments, she added, "He is seeing Susanna Chupp."

"Of course he's not," Esther said. "I'm sure Susanna has a crush on him, but that's as far as it grows."

A little spark of hope flickered within Hannah. "Do you think so?"

"*Jah*, I do. Hannah, why can't you admit that you're in love with Noah?"

Hannah walked somewhat unsteadily to the table and put her head in her hands. "I was once," she said.

"Hannah, it was an accident," Esther said gently. "It wasn't Noah's fault, and all this time you've had unforgiveness in your heart. Should you speak to the bishop?"

"The bishop?" Hannah shrieked. "Why should I speak to the bishop? I haven't done anything wrong. You sound like *Datt*."

That night was Hannah's first night back in her old bedroom, now that she could walk up the steps without being encumbered by the heavy cast. She had been looking forward to the first night back in her own bed, but sleep eluded her. She tossed and turned and was unable to escape from the thoughts that assailed her.

Was she still in love with Noah? And if so, would it do her any good because he was dating Susanna? And if he was in love with Susanna, why did she care? Surely her love for Noah had died with the accident.

Or had it?

By morning, the long sleepless night of soul

searching and prayer had, however, forced a decision; she would speak to the bishop.

Bishop William Graber ushered Hannah inside and indicated that she should sit down.

Hannah had always known him to be a kindly man, as well as wise. Hannah bit back a smile, knowing that some of the *youngie* said that the *Englischers* would mistake the bishop for their Santa Claus, given his twinkling blue eyes, round face, and gray beard.

Mrs. Fannie Graber scurried into the room and deposited mugs of hot meadow tea and a plate of food next to her husband and Hannah. "*Hullo*, Hannah. You're looking pale, dear. Now don't mind me. I'm off to finish the wash, now that the day is warming up somewhat. I hope you enjoy these baked beans with anchovy Whoopie Pies."

Hannah did her best not to look shocked. Mrs. Graber was well known throughout the community for her strange food experimentations. Why, she had even added ketchup to her church spread on one occasion.

After a moment of prayer, the bishop spoke. "I see you are no longer wearing the cast. How is your leg doing, Hannah?"

"It's getting better, *denki*." Hannah noted that the bishop did not select any food from the plate.

"And your *schweschders*? How are they doing?"

"Much better, *denki*."

Hannah nervously twisted the mug of meadow tea

round in her hands. She didn't know how to broach the subject with the bishop.

"Now, Hannah, tell me why you have come to see me today. Take your time," he added kindly.

Hannah shifted in her seat. "I have the sin of unforgiveness in my heart," she blurted out. Hannah looked at the bishop, expecting him to look shocked or at least surprised, but the expression on his face did not change. It suddenly dawned on her that the bishop would hear all sorts of sins and problems.

The bishop leaned forward. "Tell me all about it, Hannah." His tone was encouraging and warm. "We have all sinned and fallen short of the glory of *Gott*. We must strive not to sin on a daily basis," he added.

Hannah nodded. "I have unforgiveness in my heart for Noah Hostetler for causing the accident that injured not only me, but my three sisters as well. I've tried to forgive him, but I feel resentment toward him too."

The bishop nodded. "You know, of course, that it was an accident. He hadn't been speeding. He lost control of the car in the heavy mist and on the icy road. He was on *rumspringa* too."

Hannah sighed. "*Jah*, I know all that. I know Noah didn't run into our buggy on purpose. It's just that he has been the cause of so much hardship for me and my *familye*."

The bishop nodded again. "Have you asked *Gott* to help you forgive him?"

Hannah nodded. *"Jah."* She looked down, shamefaced.

"Did you know that the middle letter of the *Englisch* word *pride* is I?"

Hannah looked at the bishop in surprise. She had no idea what he meant.

"You know what *Gelassenheit* means, Hannah?" the bishop continued.

"It means submission?" Hannah asked, not sure if it had some other particular meaning that the bishop was referring to.

"*Jah*, but it means to submit to *Gott's* will. It means to resign yourself to *Gott's* will, to have a quiet spirit of self-denial and contentment."

The bishop sipped his tea, while Hannah tried to process his words. "Do you mean that I'm to accept the accident as *Gott's* will, and not blame Noah for it?"

The bishop did not answer directly, but nodded to a large, thick book on the table nearby. "See that book."

"*Jah*, the *Martyrs' Mirror*." Hannah knew the book well. Just about every Amish home she had ever been in had that book and she heard about the martyrs just about every time she was in church.

The bishop stood up and walked over to the table to fetch the book, before he sat down with it on his knee. "And do you know the full title?"

Hannah did know the full title, but she was nervous talking to the bishop, so had to collect her thoughts for a moment before she answered. *"The Martyrs' Mirror of the Defenseless Christians who baptized only upon confession of faith, and who suf-*

fered and died for the testimony of Jesus, their Savior, from the time of Christ to the year A.D. 1660."

The bishop patted the book. "And do you know why they were called *Defenseless*?"

Hannah shook her head. "No, not really."

"They were called *Defenseless* because they did not fight against authority when it was unjust."

Hannah did not see what that had to do with unforgiveness, so waited for the bishop to explain further.

"Not resisting is the same as forgiveness," the bishop continued. "*Gott* forgave us, so we must forgive others. It is not an option."

Hannah knew that in theory, but she was finding it hard to put into practice.

"Hannah," the bishop said softly, "you do not have the right *not* to forgive; that is the right of *Gott*, and *Gott* only."

Hannah nodded. Its very sense stuck at her soul.

"And you know how important forgiveness is in *The Lord's Prayer*."

Hannah silently recited *The Lord's Prayer* to herself.

Our Father, who art in heaven.
Hallowed be thy name.
Thy kingdom come, thy will be done.
On earth as it is in heaven.
Give us this day our daily bread,
and forgive us our trespasses,
as we forgive those who trespass against us.

And lead us not into temptation,
but deliver us from evil:
for thine is the kingdom,
and the power,
and the glory, forever.
Amen.

"Why, yes." Hannah felt as if a huge load had lifted off her. How could she have been so blind? She always said *The Lord's Prayer* silently before every meal, and recited it before every church meeting, so how had she overlooked the words *forgive us our trespasses, as we forgive those who trespass against us* for so long?

"As you struggle to forgive," the bishop continued, "you open yourself up to the grace of *Gott*. No one is able to forgive without *Gott's* help; it is beyond us, and so we must reply on *Gott* with a gentle and quiet spirit. If *Gott* could forgive us, how can we refuse to forgive others? At the moment you forgive, that is the moment you let your pain go. Hand it over to *Gott*." He paused for a moment. "Am I making sense?"

Hannah nodded. "Yes, *denki*."

"I am not saying you forget what happened. Yes, it was an accident. Noah had not been speeding. But what if he *had* been speeding on his *rumspringa*? Should you forgive him any less? *Nee*. No matter what, you must take all your unforgiveness, all your anger, all your resentment, and hand it over to *Gott*. It is *Gott's* business; it is not *your* business."

The bishop looked at Hannah who nodded. He

went on. "There is but one judge, and that is *Gott*. Unforgiveness is a form of judgment. Every time you feel anger, forgiveness, or resentment, you at once must give it to *Gott*, even if it is many times in the one day, even if it is many times, day after day."

Hannah finally spoke. "It does seem easy when you put it that way."

The bishop smiled. "It *is* easy, Hannah. It is easy because there is no other way. You must forgive, and you must hand over your resentment to *Gott*, again and again if necessary."

"*Denki*. *Denki* so much. I wish I'd come to you sooner."

The bishop smiled a wry smile. "Perhaps you should have listened to the ministers who say this all the time."

Hannah was at once ashamed, but looked up to see the bishop smiling at her again.

"Now, before we pray, is there anything else you would like to speak to me about?" He smiled encouragingly.

Hannah hesitated. She had been going to tell the bishop that she was conflicted about her feelings for Noah, her feelings of love for him, while at the same time having feelings of resentment for him. Yet now that she had released her sin of unforgiveness to *Gott*, there was no conflict in her heart any more.

"Nee, denki," she said slowly. "I think that it is all okay now."

The bishop smiled. "*Gut*. Then let us pray."

After prayer, the bishop showed Hannah to the

door. "Remember, Hannah," he said, "No matter how great our sins or our problems, *Gott* will always show us the way home."

"Denki," Hannah said meekly.

As she walked down the porch steps, she heard the bishop say, *"Liebe macht erfinderisch." Love will find a way.*

Hannah looked back. Did the bishop know about her feelings for Noah?

Chapter Nineteen

Hannah felt physically lighter ever since she had spoken to the bishop. The bishop's words had hit home and she had handed over all her unforgiveness to *Gott*. In fact, looking back, she wondered why she'd ever had unforgiveness in her heart in the first place. Of course, as Hannah thought with a chuckle, she was physically lighter as well, due to the fact that her cast had been removed.

Hannah had hoped to happen across Noah ever since she had spoken to the bishop, but the next Sunday meeting wasn't until the Sunday after the coming one, and Noah had not gone into his *mudder's* quilt shop again, at least not while Hannah was there. She spent much of her time daydreaming about what would happen when she saw him again.

Hannah had also escaped the unpleasantness of spending another day with Mrs. Yoder at the schoolhouse, as Mary Knepp had recovered sooner than expected and was back teaching the school children.

Hannah returned home one night after her morning in the quilt shop followed by a visit to Rebecca in the hospital. Hannah was in high spirits, as Rebecca was improving far better than the doctors had hoped. In fact, the doctors had promised to discharge her soon.

However, Hannah's mood soon changed. As she was helping her *mudder* prepare dinner, her *mudder* turned to her. "Now listen, Hannah. Beth Yoder has invited you for dinner tomorrow night."

"Nee, Mamm!" Hannah's eyes went wide. "Please, I told you that I don't like David Yoder at all." Hannah considered telling her *mudder* that David had tried to kiss her, but then decided against it. Beth Yoder was a close friend of her *mudder's*, and Hannah didn't want to say anything that would possibly put a strain on that relationship.

Mrs. Miller held up her hand. "*Nee*, Hannah, listen. I don't think it's like that at all. We didn't discuss it, but I think Beth has realized that you feel uncomfortable around her son, David. She liked speaking to you the day you both taught together and she wants to stay friends with you. In fact, she hasn't even invited you to her own *haus* for dinner."

"She hasn't?" Hannah was puzzled.

"*Nee*. She's invited you to have dinner with her in a restaurant."

"A restaurant?" Hannah parroted. Mr. and Mrs. Yoder were known to be far stricter than all the other members of the Amish community to which the Millers belonged. In fact, Jessie Yoder always wore her bonnet over her *kapp* in public, without exception.

"Jah."

"That seems a bit strange, *Mamm*." Hannah had an uneasy feeling. Why on earth would Beth Yoder want to meet her at a restaurant? She didn't think the Yoders even approved of *Englisch* restaurants. Perhaps Beth was going to attempt to talk her into dating David?

Mrs. Miller simply shrugged, and continued the preparation of dinner.

Hannah sat in the restaurant, looking around at the other patrons. She was the only Amish person there, although she knew that some of the other members of her community did on occasion eat at this restaurant. The clock on the wall showed that Mrs. Yoder was late. The table for two had been reserved, and Hannah had taken the seat facing the entrance so that Mrs. Yoder would find her more easily.

Hannah studied the menu while she was waiting, and decided she would order chicken pot pie with a side of chow chow, or perhaps something with mashed potatoes, pepper slaw, and creamed celery.

Mrs. Yoder's full of surprises, Hannah thought. *I know Amish cooks don't work here, but Amish cooks do work at another restaurant just a block from here. Plus this restaurant seems more one suited to dating couples, rather than for friends. The other one's more suited to that. I wonder why she chose this one?*

Hannah shrugged and looked at her surroundings. The lighting was dimmed, and the walls were a pale golden amber color that reflected the soft glow of the candlelight from the ornate candles on each table. The napkins, by way of contrast, were a deep burgundy.

Hannah looked at the door once again. There was still no sign of Mrs. Yoder. Had her *mudder* got the restaurant's name right? *Yes,* Hannah thought, *there was a reservation here in the name of Yoder.*

"Hannah." The voice was masculine. It was not Mrs. Yoder's voice at all.

Hannah looked up into the face of David Yoder.

"David!" Hannah realized she had said the word with some horror, but didn't really care. "What are *you* doing here?"

David sat down in the chair opposite Hannah's. "*Mamm* said to say *sorry*. She couldn't come at the last minute, so she sent me instead."

It all became obvious to Hannah. This was a setup! Mrs. Yoder had never had any intention of having dinner with her. It had simply been a ploy to get Hannah to have dinner with David.

Hannah abruptly stood up. "I'll be leaving then, David."

"Nee, nee," David said, his brows meeting in a frown. "I wanted to have dinner with you to apologize anyway. Please, will you forgive me for my behavior, Hannah?"

Hannah's heart softened and she sat back down. Perhaps *Gott* was testing her over the matter of forgiveness. She had forgiven Noah, and now she had to forgive David too. Besides, it was a public place, and he was hardly going to try to kiss her again here.

"*Jah*, I forgive you, David. However, I will only agree to have dinner with you if you understand that I will *not* be dating you. Not now, not ever!" Hannah thought that came out a little harshly, but she didn't want to lead him on.

Hannah saw something that looked like a momentary flash of anger pass across David's face, but then he agreed. "*Jah, jah*. I'm so happy you've forgiven me, Hannah." He smiled a wide smile, which Hannah thought looked quite fake and insincere. Nevertheless, she had learned her lesson about forgiveness and was determined to follow through. She would be gracious and have dinner with David Yoder.

However, instead of pleasant conversation, David bombarded Hannah with questions: who had she dated in the past, was she interested in anyone now, how long did she intend to work for Mrs. Hostetler. Hannah managed to deflect all the questions, but only with some difficulty. David also criticized Noah Hostetler, but Hannah did not respond, as she figured he did so only to draw some kind of reaction from her. He did not ask how her leg was, or ask after her *schweschders*.

"What time did you say the taxi was calling for you?" David asked between courses.

"Eight thirty, David. That's the second time you've asked."

David smiled. "I'm just looking out for you, Hannah. I wouldn't want you to miss your ride, with you relying on taxis given how you feel about buggies and all. Do you think you'll have time for dessert after all?"

"*Jah*, I sure will." If Hannah was going to be forced to wait until eight thirty in David's company, she was going to do her best to enjoy it, and that was going to mean eating dessert. "Besides," she said aloud, "if I did miss that taxi, I'd simply call another."

Hannah noted the look of worry on David's face. *Why is he so keen to have me leave at eight thirty?* she wondered. "I *will* be leaving at eight thirty, anyway," she said, more to herself than to David. "If the dessert is late coming, I will simply not eat all of it."

David nodded with clear relief. "You are a beautiful woman, Hannah," he said, at the same time reaching across and patting her hand.

Hannah looked up in shock, and to her horror, looked straight into the eyes of Noah Hostetler. They held each other's gaze for a moment, and Hannah was so surprised that she did not think to snatch her hand away until Noah had turned on his heel and left the restaurant.

What have I done? Hannah's heart thumped loudly and her throat tightened. *Noah will think I'm dating David Yoder.*

As if through a mist, she vaguely heard David order hot apple fritters with ice cream. "And you, miss?"

Hannah looked up at the waitress. "Shoo-Fly pie, please," she said automatically.

David peered into her face. "Have I upset you?"

"*Nee*, well, not exactly, David. But you mustn't say things like that. And please do not touch my hand again."

David simply nodded and looked around the room, and then at his watch. Hannah was surprised to see that he was wearing a watch, as she knew that Mr. and Mrs. Yoder did not approve of them. It looked like a fancy watch too, not that Hannah knew anything about watches.

Hannah was only able to have a mouthful or two of the Shoo-Fly pie, as her stomach was churning. She had finally forgiven Noah and come to terms with her feelings for him, but now he no doubt thought she was dating David. Then another thought occurred to her. What was Noah doing here anyway? Was he meeting someone, perhaps a girl? Was it true that he was seeing *Englisch* girls after all?

Hannah sank into the depths of despair. Despite being seated close to the roaring fire, she felt a chill run through her veins.

Finally, the clock on the wall told her it was eight twenty-five. "*Denki*, David. I'll be going now."

David made to rise but Hannah waved him down. She had no wish for him to wait outside with her. She didn't want a repeat performance of the incident in the barn the other week. "*Nee*, David, stay and finish your dessert. The taxi will be here for me any moment."

To her relief, he readily agreed. Hannah hurried outside to see that the taxi had just pulled up. She slid into the seat with a sigh as she released all her pent-up tension. Hannah had made up her mind to tell her parents about David, how he had tried to kiss her. That was the only way to stop dinners being arranged behind her back. In fact, it would put a sure stop to all matchmaking ideas of Mrs. Yoder's as well as her *mudder's*.

The taxi driver looked over his shoulder at Hannah. "If you're not in a hurry, miss, could you wait five minutes? I have another ride booked for eight thirty-five—she lives near you."

"Sure, that's fine." Hannah didn't mind at all. The taxi was warm, and besides, it gave her the opportunity to think about what she would say to her parents. It might even give her time to think how she could put things right with Noah, if that were even possible.

Hannah was looking out the window of the taxi when she saw David come out of the restaurant. He stood there, looking around. Hannah sunk back in the seat, and was relieved that David hadn't caught sight of her. Just then a short, shapely *Englisch* girl hurried over to him. She was wearing a short skirt and an abundance of jewelry. She flung her arms around David's neck and kissed him hard.

Hannah's jaw dropped open. She couldn't stop staring, despite her shock at the scene unfolding in front of her. David and the *Englisch* girl were embroiled in a lengthy, passionate embrace right there on the street. *He must've been pretending to be interested in me just to throw his* mudder *off the track*, Hannah thought with astonishment.

* * *

Noah hurried away from the restaurant. His worst fears appeared to have come true; his beloved Hannah was having dinner with David Yoder. Why, the *mann* even had his hand on Hannah's and she didn't look as if she minded. What on earth was going on?

Chapter Twenty

Hannah's *mudder* looked up, pleased with herself. "So how was dinner, Hannah? Did you have a *gut* time?"

Hannah took off her thick coat and looked around. "*Nee*, *Mamm*, not at all. Are Esther and Martha asleep?"

Her *daed* nodded. *"Jah."*

"I'd like to talk to you both, please."

Her parents exchanged glances. Hannah walked over to the table and sat down. "Mrs. Yoder did not come. Instead, David Yoder came."

"He did?" Her *daed* looked straight at Mrs. Miller, who avoided his gaze.

Hannah pressed on. "*Jah*, Mrs. Yoder had no intention of coming. David admitted as much."

Mrs. Miller spoke up. "Hannah, why won't you give David a chance?"

Hannah shook her head at her *mudder*, frustrated. "You don't understand, *Mamm*. It's not just that I've never felt anything for David, it's that…" Her voice trailed away.

"Go on, Hannah," her *daed* said, with encouragement in his voice.

"Well, I didn't want to say before, *Mamm*, as you're close friends with Mrs. Yoder, but David tried to kiss me in the Yoders' barn after I was over there for dinner."

Mr. Miller looked shocked, but Mrs. Miller asked, "Are you sure?"

"I could hardly mistake something like that, *Mamm*. Plus, it was the second time he tried. This time he tried much harder than the first time—I had to slam my crutches on his foot to get away from him."

Mr. Miller gasped and Mrs. Miller's hand flew to her mouth.

"Not only that, when I left tonight, I was sitting in the taxi while the driver was waiting for someone else, and I saw David kissing an *Englisch* girl," Hannah continued. "He was kissing her right in the street, in front of everyone. I mean they were *really* kissing each other. Plus she barely had any clothes on, even in this weather."

Her parents' jaws dropped open. "Are you sure?" her *mudder* asked again, her face ashen.

"Of course she's sure, Rachel." Mr. Miller shook his head. "You've done the right thing in telling us, Hannah. There will be no more matchmaking attempts; I can assure you of that." He looked at Mrs. Miller when he spoke.

Hannah looked at her *Mamm* to see her reaction, and to her relief, she nodded. "*Nee*, Hannah, of course not. I won't mention this to Beth, but I'll certainly make sure that you do not have to suffer David Yoder again."

"Denki, Mamm."

"I'll make you a nice hot cup of meadow tea and fetch you some Whoopie Pies."

Mrs. Miller hurried off to the kitchen. Hannah knew that her *mudder* was sorry for her part in this, and was trying to make it up to her with food, which was her way of showing affection.

When her *mudder* was out of earshot, Mr. Miller spoke to Hannah in a conspiratorial tone. "I sent Noah to that restaurant tonight to deliver the two oak, bow-backed high chairs for *kinner* that they'd ordered. Did you happen to see him there?"

Oh great, now both my parents are matchmakers, Hannah thought. Aloud she said, "*Jah*, and he saw me having dinner with David Yoder."

"Oh." Mr. Miller looked crestfallen.

That night, Hannah tossed and turned in bed. *Will I ever get a good night's sleep?* she asked herself. On the one hand, David Yoder was not going to be a problem for her anymore, but on the other hand, Noah clearly thought that there was something going on between her and David. No doubt he would find out in time, but would that be too late? And what if Noah had no feelings for her any more? What if he had never had any feelings for her in the first place? Had she been mistaken all along?

Hannah sat up, put the pillow over her face and lay back down. She sent up a silent and urgent prayer to *Gott* to ask Him to help her.

Hannah finally gave up trying to sleep. She thought a glass of warm milk might help, so she crept down the stairs so as not to wake her sisters. Rebecca was snoring loudly, and Esther wasn't stirring.

Making the warm milk distracted Hannah somewhat, so by the time she sat down at the kitchen table to drink her milk, she felt somewhat better.

She started when a voice came from the doorway. "Hannah! Why are you awake at this time of night?"

Hannah smiled at Esther. "I could ask you the same thing, or did I wake you?"

Esther shook her head and then nodded. "It must've been you. But don't worry about it. What's wrong?"

"Nothing," Hannah said dismissively.

"I think I'll have some warm milk, if that's all right?" Esther gingerly lowered herself into the chair.

Hannah jumped up. "Sure. It won't take me long."

Soon the two sisters were sitting opposite each other, sipping their hot milk. "You still haven't told me what's wrong," Esther said. When Hannah didn't answer, she said, "Noah."

Hannah felt her face burn all the way to the tips of her ears. "It's difficult."

"Only if you make it difficult," Esther said. "The two of you were in love before the accident."

She would have said more, but Hannah interrupted her. "You don't know that, do you? Not how

Noah felt, I mean. I was in love with him but he never said he was in love with me."

Esther pulled a face. "Of course he was and he still is."

Hannah shook her head. "You have no way of knowing."

"Shoo-Fly Pie!" Esther suddenly said.

Hannah wasn't sure if she heard her correctly. "What did you say?"

"I'm starving. Hannah, would you mind fetching me a piece of Shoo-Fly Pie please?"

Hannah dutifully went to the gas refrigerator and took out the Shoo-Fly Pie. She cut a large piece and put it on a plate for Esther. "Now, is there anything else while I'm on my feet? I want to sit down and relax."

Esther chuckled. "Doesn't it make you hungry when you wake up in the middle of the night? You might as well have some too."

Hannah sighed with resignation and scooped a piece onto a plate for herself. She hoped the Shoo-Fly Pie had distracted Esther from the subject of Noah and at first it seemed she was right.

"The wet bottom pies are my favorite," Esther said, "and with cupcakes, I only like to eat the frosting. So where were we? Oh yes, Noah."

Hannah groaned. "I said he was dating Susanna. Did I say that? I can't remember. I'm too tired to think straight. Jessie Yoder told me he was."

"Of course he's not dating Susanna. What nonsense," Esther said. "I don't trust David Yoder and

I don't trust his sister Jessie either. I'm sure they're working together. Anyway, I'm certain that's not true," Esther said. "I'm sure Jacob would have told me."

Hannah was surprised. "Have you seen Jacob lately?"

Esther stopped, her spoon halfway to her mouth. "Did I forget to tell you? He was here yesterday."

"What did he say?" Hannah asked Esther.

Esther studied her spoon. "Well, he'd just said how the farm was going and how his *bruders* were. What you mean especially?"

"Did he say anything about Noah?" Hannah said.

Esther tapped her chin. "*Jah*, I asked him how Noah was and he said Noah was sad and alone."

Hannah sat bolt upright. "Really? Sad and alone?"

"Joshua didn't use those words exactly," Esther said, "but reading between the lines, Noah is sad and alone. I'm sure Jacob would have told me if Noah was dating anyone."

Hannah thought there was probably more to the story and was about to ask when Esther spoke again. "Anyway, Hannah, why are you so interested? Does that mean you've finally forgiven Noah? You never did tell me how your talk with the bishop went."

Hannah put her head in her hands. "*Jah*, I've forgiven Noah, but I don't think he wants me anymore. I think I've left it too late. I don't know what I think. One moment I think one thing and one moment I think the other, and it's all too much for me," she said.

"It will be all right. You'll see."

Hannah wished she shared her *schweschder's* confidence.

The next day, Hannah arrived to work at Katie Hostetler's quilt shop. Katie met her at the door, clearly excited. "Hannah, yesterday I sold your double wedding ring quilt!"

When Katie named the price, Hannah gasped. "Oh *denki*, Mrs. Hostetler. That will be a big help to my *familye*."

Katie took a long look at Hannah. "Are you all right? You look like you could do with a mug of *kaffi*. Come on through; we have time before we open for the day."

"*Denki*, Katie." Hannah followed Mrs. Hostetler through to the little room at the back of the shop.

Katie poured Hannah a mug of *kaffi*, and then sat down opposite her. "Hannah, are you sure you're not sad about selling your double wedding ring quilt? You should have kept it for your marriage."

Hannah shook her head. "*Nee*, Katie. I don't think I'll ever get married." The words were out before Hannah could stop them. She had forgotten for a moment that Katie was Noah's *mudder*. Thankfully, Katie did not question her, and the two sat in a somewhat uncomfortable silence while they drank their *kaffi*.

Later, Katie went out to run an errand and Hannah was busy piecing a quilt on the foot-operated, treadle sewing machine. She had just stopped to fill a bobbin when she heard the door open. Hannah stood up and looked at the *mann* who had just entered.

To her surprise, it was Noah. "*Hullo*, Noah," she stammered, as she stood up.

"*Hiya*, Hannah."

The two just stood there looking at each other. Hannah studied Noah's eyes for any sign of affection for her, but all she could detect was the intensity in his expression. She had no idea what it meant.

"Oh *gut*, you're off your crutches now."

"Jah." Hannah smiled at Noah.

"How are your *schweschders* doing?"

"*Gut, denki.* Esther and Martha are much better, and Rebecca's coming home any day." Hannah tried to speak evenly and hoped the tremors she was feeling did not show in her voice.

"Wunderbar!" Noah beamed at her.

Hannah's heart was thumping so hard she felt it would beat right out of her chest.

"Jessie Yoder was at our house the other day," Noah began, but Hannah interrupted him.

"To see Jacob?"

Noah gave Hannah an inquiring look. "*Jah*, well, at least I think that was why, although she came to bring a message from her *mudder*."

Hannah nodded. *Oh no, just as I suspected! I thought Jessie Yoder had her eyes on Jacob. Poor Esther will be so upset.* Hannah looked at Noah to continue, but he shifted from one foot to the other and looked most uncomfortable.

"Jessie said that you were at the Yoders' house for dinner recently." The hurt in Noah's eyes was unmistakable.

"Nee!" Hannah exclaimed.

Noah looked puzzled. "You weren't?"

Hannah shook her head. "Well, *jah*, I was, but…"

Hannah was interrupted by Katie coming back through the store door. Katie came to an abrupt halt when she saw Hannah and Noah talking. No one spoke for a moment, and then Katie said, "Sorry to interrupt. I was just going through to the back room."

"I was just leaving, *Mamm*." With that, Noah nodded to Hannah and left.

Hannah returned to the sewing machine, and bent her head over the bobbin so that Katie would not see the tears freely falling down her cheeks. Noah thought she and David were seeing each other. She had the opportunity to set him straight, but hadn't found the words in time.

Oh Gott, *why are You testing me like this?* she asked silently through her tears.

Noah shook his head as he hurried away from his one true love. *Why did I even go to* Mamm's *store to see Hannah?* he asked himself. *Hannah admitted that she'd been at the Yoders'* haus *for dinner. Plus I saw her with my very own eyes having dinner with David Yoder at the restaurant.* Still, Noah felt that he and Hannah were truly meant for each other, but that would mean there was another explanation for what he had seen, and what other possible explanation could there be?

Later that afternoon, Noah was putting the finishing touches to a set of steam bent dining chairs. He was removing the clamps when Mr. Miller walked over to him. He liked Mr. Miller—he was a fair boss, and even more than that, he was a friend. The two of them often chatted amiably through the day. Noah had a lot of respect for Mr. Miller, and Mr. Miller clearly held no resentment for him over the accident that had injured his four *dochders*.

Mr. Miller inspected the chairs. "They're looking fine. They've turned out well." He rubbed his chin, looked at Noah, and then looked at the chairs again.

"Jah." Noah wondered why Mr. Miller appeared nervous.

"Did you happen to see Hannah when you visited your *mudder's* store today?"

Noah nodded, uncomfortable with the memory. "Only briefly, though."

Mr. Miller nodded. "Hannah is a little upset at the moment," he said, "although of course she wouldn't like me saying that."

Noah was dismayed. "Upset? With me?" he asked, his heart in his mouth.

"*Nee*, *nee*," Mr. Miller said, patting Noah on the shoulder, "with her *mudder*. You know how women are. It seems my *fraa*, Rachel, and her friend, Beth Yoder, thought that Hannah and David Yoder should be betrothed, and they've taken measures toward that end."

"Really?" *Could that be all it was?* Noah wondered. He hoped with all his heart that it was so.

"*Jah*. They even pretended that Beth wanted to meet Hannah for dinner at a restaurant, but they sent

David along instead." Mr. Miller nodded awkwardly and then walked away, muttering to himself about a missing pot of wax, saying he couldn't remember where he'd put it.

Noah was left alone with his thoughts. His spirits were lifted by the fact that Mr. Miller clearly approved of the possibility of him having a relationship with Hannah, but did Mr. Miller really have all the facts? Only the other day, Jessie Yoder himself had told him that David was dating Hannah. Had David put Jessie up to it, or was it the truth?

There was only one thing for it. The next time Noah saw Hannah, he would have to ask her, no matter how uncomfortable and awkward it might turn out to be. At least he would know, once and for all, whether there was any hope for him.

Chapter Twenty-One

Hannah was utterly overwrought. She was finding all the work too much, and had no time to herself to think and pray, or even to get her thoughts in some sort of order. There were all the chores at home, plus looking after Esther and Martha. Sure, Mary had taken most of that burden, but Hannah still had to work for Katie Hostetler in the quilt store three mornings a week, and visit Rebecca in the hospital most afternoons as well. Hannah loved looking after her sisters and visiting Rebecca, and enjoyed working for Mrs. Hostetler. She even enjoyed most of her chores, but she did need some space to get her thoughts together.

The following afternoon, instead of going home after visiting Rebecca in the hospital, Hannah escaped to the fields to have some time alone and to pour out her heart to *Gott*.

"*Denki* for working on my heart, *Gott*," she said

aloud. "*Denki* for the fact that I don't have unforgiveness in my heart any more."

Hannah sat and looked over the frozen pond, enjoying the quiet chill of the afternoon. The landscape before her was lovely in its simplicity. The familiar *chick-a-dee-dee-dee* call of the black-capped chickadee caused her to look up. Six or so chickadees were perched on a branch in a nearby tree. The tree's branches were covered with white frosting.

Soon, the familiar clip clop of a horse's shoes broke the silence. Hannah looked over to her right side and saw Noah's big black gelding ambling into view from the direction of her *haus*.

Noah must be on his way home from work, she thought, with a momentary pang of alarm. Would he stop? If he did, what would she say? *I will have to set things right with him*, Hannah thought. *I will have to tell him that I forgive him, and that I'm not dating David Yoder.*

Hannah ran through what she could say, yet a feeling of disquiet had settled in her stomach. What if Noah didn't have feelings for her after all, and didn't care that she wasn't dating David Yoder? What if he really was dating Susanna? That would prove awfully embarrassing for Hannah. Nee, *I must still tell him*, Hannah thought. *I also have to tell him that I forgive him. I owe him that much.*

Hannah's heart was in her mouth as she watched the buggy approach. As it slowed down, her heart beat faster and her mouth ran dry.

The buggy came to a stop and Noah jumped

down. "Hannah! What are you doing out here, alone in the cold?" he called out.

Hannah simply waved and waited for Noah to come closer. What happened next seemed to Hannah to happen in slow motion. Noah was approaching her, his eyes on hers. He did not see the fallen branch in front of him. Noah tripped hard over the fallen branch and fell through the air toward the pond, his arms flung out to the side.

Hannah stood and watched the scene unfold in horror, her cry frozen in her throat. Coming to her senses, she ran over to Noah, who had fallen into the ice.

Mercifully, he was right next to the shore, but appeared to be unconscious. Hannah dragged on his legs to try to get him out, but he was too heavy, and she fell backward, his boot in her hands. "Help, me, *Gott*; help me, *Gott*," she cried.

After what seemed an age, Hannah was finally able to drag Noah out of the icy water and onto the bank. She bent over him, calling his name, but he didn't open his eyes. It was then that Hannah saw the nasty, bleeding bump near his temple.

Hannah tried to drag him over to the *familye* buggy, but only managed to drag him a foot or so, so exhausted was she from dragging him from the icy water. As there was no way Hannah could get Noah to the buggy, she ran to the buggy and seized the large, warm quilt sitting on the seat.

She ran back and put it over Noah, tucking it under and around him. She took off her cloak and gently put it under his head as a pillow. Then she ran back to the buggy as fast as she could. Hannah took the reins and passed them through the window, and then climbed in the buggy.

She turned the buggy around, and once the horse was facing straight, clicked him on. The big black gelding took off into a sound trot, but Hannah yelled, "Get up!" At her urging, the horse took off at a strange gait. Hannah felt frightened at first, until she realized that this horse was a former harness racer, unlike her own Saddlebred, Rock. While her own horse had a high gait, this horse was pacing, and from where Hannah was sitting, the horse rocking from side to side was a strange sight. To Hannah's relief, he was going awfully fast and appeared to be sure-footed.

She reached her *haus* in no time, calling loudly to her parents as she got out of the buggy. Her *mudder* ran out of the door of the *haus* just as her father ran over from the barn. Hannah registered the look on their faces; both had their mouths gaping wide.

"Hannah, you're driving a buggy! Noah's buggy! What's happened?" her *daed* yelled urgently.

Oh, I drove the buggy, Hannah thought with a little surprise, but it was as if this were all happening to someone else and she were watching it all unfold. It all seemed so surreal. "*Datt*, Noah's had an accident! He's unconscious and he hit his head and fell in the pond and there's blood," she said all in one breath.

Her *mudder's* hand flew to her mouth.

"Quick, Rachel, go to the barn and call for the

doktor. Tell him to hurry!" Mr. Miller ran to the buggy and Hannah jumped in beside him.

In no time they were back at Noah's side. To Hannah's immense relief, he was stirring and trying to speak.

Hannah and her *daed* managed to get Noah into the buggy. As Noah had regained consciousness, he was able to lean on both of them, which made their job easier.

Mr. Miller drove more steadily back to the *haus*, and he helped Hannah get Noah inside, where they lay him down on one of the mattresses in the living room, by the potbelly stove. Mrs. Miller piled quilts onto him and Mr. Miller stoked the fire.

Hannah and both her parents stood over Noah, looking at him. His eyes were open, but he wasn't saying anything. He looked dazed. "The *doktor's* coming right away," Mrs. Miller said. "I called Katie Hostetler at her quilt store, but she didn't answer. She must have left for the day."

Mr. Miller turned to Hannah. "Hannah, you'll have to go to the Hostetler's *haus* and tell them what's happened. Drive carefully and don't rush. Noah is going to be okay. See, he's getting color back in his face already."

"Jah, Datt." Hannah did not want to leave Noah, but someone had to fetch his *mudder*, and besides, her parents were better able to take care of Noah than she was.

Without thinking, Hannah went outside into the cold and once again took up the reins.

Chapter Twenty-Two

When Hannah drove up to the Hostetlers' house, the first person she saw was Jacob, who was shocked to see her driving the buggy. He too stood there with his mouth open, speechless. She jumped from out of the buggy and called to him. "Jacob, Noah's fallen into the pond and hit his head, and we've called for the *doktor. Datt* says he'll be all right, though. I've come to get your *mudder*."

Hannah held the horse while Jacob ran inside the *haus*. He quickly returned with his *mudder*, Katie Hostetler. "Hannah, you're driving the buggy!" she exclaimed. "What happened to Noah?"

"He tripped over and hit his head and fell in the pond," Hannah said breathlessly. "The *doktor* will likely be there at our *haus* with him by now. I've come to get you."

Katie clutched at her throat. "How bad is he?"

"*Datt* says he'll be all right."

Katie nodded, and then sent Jacob to go find her

husband. The two women drove back to the Millers' *haus* in silence. Despite her *daed's* words, Hannah was sick with worry about Noah. *I must tell him I've forgiven him*, she thought.

When Hannah eased the horse to a stop outside her *haus*, the *doktor* and Mr. Miller had Noah supported between them and were heading out of the *haus* toward the *doktor's* car. The *doktor* addressed Katie. "Mrs. Hostetler, Noah might have a mild concussion. I'm taking him to the hospital to be checked out, just to be on the safe side. There's no cause for alarm. This is regular in the case of a suspected concussion. Would you like to come, too?"

"*Jah*, of course." Katie hurried over to Noah.

"Hannah?" he whispered.

Katie turned to the *doktor*. "Can Hannah come with us?"

"Yes, of course. There's plenty of room."

Hannah looked questioningly at her parents. "*Jah*, you go, Hannah," her *daed* said. "I'll rub down Noah's horse and put him in the barn. Katie, when your husband gets here, I'll tell him what's happened."

Katie nodded to Mr. Miller. "*Denki*, Abraham."

Mr. Miller and the *doktor* helped Noah into the backseat of the *doktor's* car and fastened his seat belt around him. Katie climbed into the front seat of the car, leaving Hannah to sit in the back with Noah.

Noah leaned his head on Hannah's shoulder and she held her breath. On the one hand, she was enjoying Noah's proximity to her, but on the other hand, she was so dreadfully worried about him. Noah reached out and took Hannah's hand. She clasped his hand, wondering if he knew what he was doing. Was this simply a side effect of the concussion?

When they reached the hospital, a bossy-looking nurse whisked Noah away in a wheelchair. Hannah was left alone while Katie went outside to wait for her husband.

After some time, the nurse returned. "Are you Hannah Miller?"

"Yes, I am."

"Noah Hostetler wants to see you. Come with me."

Hannah stood up and followed the nurse down a long, sterile corridor. "Is he okay?"

"See for yourself." The nurse smiled at her, and then opened the door to a tiny, private room.

Hannah walked through and saw Noah sitting up in a hospital bed, a bandage around his head.

"You drove the buggy," he said, smiling.

Hannah smiled and sat down on the chair next to his bed. "*Hullo* to you too." She at once felt shy.

They sat for a moment in silence, until Hannah said, "Oh, I almost forgot. I forgive you, Noah."

Noah smiled at her, causing her heart to flutter wildly. "*Denki*, Hannah."

Hannah then realized that she hadn't yet asked after him. She still felt like she was in a dream. "What did the *doktors* say? How are you feeling?"

"I didn't need any stitches in my head. They don't think I have a concussion, but I have to stay in overnight for observation. They should release me tomorrow."

Hannah nodded. *"Gut."*

Noah moved to dangle his legs over the side of the bed. "Hannah, can I ask you something?"

Hannah felt a little uneasy. What would he ask? "Sure," she said.

"Jessie Yoder's been coming to our *haus*. She wants to see Jacob, no doubt, although he does his best to avoid her attentions, but she told me that you were dating her *bruder*, David."

"Nee!" Hannah hadn't meant to speak so loudly, but she was shocked that Jessie would say such a thing. "*Nee*, Noah, that's not true at all."

Noah beamed from ear to ear. *"Gut!"*

Hannah looked at Noah. *He must have feelings for me after all*, she thought. Warmth filled her, from her toes right to the top of her head. Her cheeks flushed warm. "David has been pursuing me despite me never giving him any encouragement, and his *mudder* Beth has been trying to play matchmaker." Hannah sighed. "My *mudder* was part of the matchmaking too. Well, she was, until I told her..." Hannah broke off, embarrassed.

"Told her what?" Noah asked, leaning forward. "Hannah?" he prompted.

"Until I told her that David tried to kiss me in his barn, in the dark too."

Noah gasped.

"But I slammed my crutches into his foot, and ran back to the *haus*," Hannah added. She saw that

Noah was doing his best to keep a smile from his face at that piece of news. Then a thought occurred to Hannah. "Noah, I was helping out Mrs. Yoder at the schoolhouse one day, and she implied you were dating someone, perhaps an *Englisch* girl," she said.

It was Noah's turn to look affronted. "*Nee*, that's not true either. I haven't ever dated anyone. I certainly would never date an *Englisch* girl. Anyway, I've only ever had eyes for one girl."

Hannah looked away, unable to meet his gaze. A rush of shyness overtook her. *Does he mean me?* she wondered. *Who else could he mean? He must mean me*. Hannah wanted so hard for Noah to mean that he had only ever had eyes for her, that she couldn't quite believe it.

"It seems you are over your fear of buggies now. Is that right?"

Hannah looked into Noah's face. "*Jah*, I am." She smiled at him.

"Then you won't be afraid to come on a buggy ride with me?"

His meaning escaped Hannah for the moment. *"Nee,"* she said thoughtfully. "I'm truly over my fear of buggies now." Then it dawned on her—Noah was asking her to date him. She looked up into Noah's twinkling eyes and smiling face, barely able to contain her excitement. "Noah! Do you mean…? Do you mean…?" she stammered.

Noah didn't answer her question, but simply smiled and got out of the bed. "Hannah, will you come over to the window with me? There's something I want to show you."

Hannah followed Noah to the window, which overlooked a beautiful park. The park was in the shadows of the hospital and Hannah could see a children's playground with a jungle gym and a set of swings. Although it was near the end of winter, ribbons of silver mist wound their way around the swings.

"Mist always reminds me of that morning," said Noah, softly. "The morning I ran into your buggy. I think the memories will haunt me until the end of my days."

"And yet," Hannah said, pulling her heavy woolen cloak tight around her shoulders, even though she was indoors, "what happened on that morning is what has truly brought us together now. I know the accident wasn't your fault, Noah. I do see that now. I do know what a careful person you are, and that what happened that morning could have happened to anyone."

Just as she finished speaking, Noah moved closer to her. Suddenly his eyes were directly in front of Hannah's, and then he lowered his face toward hers, so that their foreheads pressed together.

"Are you certain you are okay, Hannah?"

Hannah wrapped her fingers around the nape of his neck. "*Jah*, I am," she assured him. Then she closed her eyes and kissed him on the nose. "How can I not be, with you here?"

The mist pressed against the hospital window.

Hannah pulled back from Noah and looked through the window for the park, which had vanished under the haze of silver. The only thing visible in her world now was Noah, though she wondered if that had not always been the case.

Noah pressed his lips against Hannah's and she melted into his kindness and warmth, certain she had never felt such peace before in her entire life, knowing this peace was hers to feel every day for the rest of her life with Noah.

* * * * *

SPECIAL EXCERPT FROM

Love Inspired®

On her way home, pregnant and alone,
an Amish woman finds herself stranded
with the last person she wanted to see.

Read on for a sneak preview of
Shelter from the Storm *by Patricia Davids,*
available September 2019 from Love Inspired.

"There won't be another bus going that way until the day after tomorrow."

"Are you sure?" Gemma Lapp stared at the agent behind the counter in stunned disbelief.

"Of course I'm sure. I work for the bus company."

She clasped her hands together tightly, praying the tears that pricked the backs of her eyes wouldn't start flowing. She couldn't afford a motel room for two nights.

She wheeled her suitcase over to the bench. Sitting down with a sigh, she moved her suitcase in front of her so she could prop up her swollen feet. After two solid days on a bus she was ready to lie down. Anywhere.

She bit her lower lip to stop it from quivering. She could place a call to the phone shack her parents shared with their Amish neighbors to let them know she was returning and ask her father to send a car for her, but she would have to leave a message.

Any message she left would be overheard. If she gave the real reason, even Jesse Crump would know before she reached home. She couldn't bear that, although she

LIEXP0819

didn't understand why his opinion mattered so much. His stoic face wouldn't reveal his thoughts, but he was sure to gloat when he learned he'd been right about her reckless ways. He had said she was looking for trouble and that she would find it sooner or later. Well, she had found it all right.

No, she wouldn't call. What she had to say was better said face-to-face. She was cowardly enough to delay as long as possible.

She didn't know how she was going to find the courage to tell her mother and father that she was six months pregnant, and Robert Troyer, the man who'd promised to marry her, was long gone.

LIEXP0819

Looking for inspiration in tales
of hope, faith and heartfelt romance?

Check out **Love Inspired**® and
Love Inspired® Suspense books!

New books available every month!

CONNECT WITH US AT:

Facebook.com/groups/HarlequinConnection

Facebook.com/HarlequinBooks

Twitter.com/HarlequinBooks

Instagram.com/HarlequinBooks

Pinterest.com/HarlequinBooks

ReaderService.com

Love Inspired®

LIGENRE2018R2

Could a pretend Christmastime courtship lead to a forever match?

Read on for a sneak preview of Her Amish Holiday Suitor, *part of Carrie Lighte's Amish Country Courtships miniseries.*

Nick took his seat next to her and picked up the reins, but before moving onward, he said, "I don't understand it, Lucy. Why is my caring about you such an awful thing?" His voice was quivering and Lucy felt a pang of guilt. She knew she was overreacting. Rather, she was reacting to a heartache that had plagued her for years, not one Nick had caused that evening.

"I don't expect you to understand," she said, wiping her rough woolen mitten across her cheeks.

"But I want to. Can't you explain it to me?"

Nick's voice was so forlorn Lucy let her defenses drop. "I've always been treated like this, my entire life. *Lucy's too weak, too fragile, too small, she can't go outside or run around or have any fun because she'll get sick. She'll stop breathing. She'll wind up in the hospital.* My whole life, Nick. And then the one little taste of utter abandon I ever experienced—charging through the dark with a frosty wind whisking against my face, feeling totally invigorated and alive... You want to take that away from me, too."

She was crying so hard her words were barely intelligible, but Nick didn't interrupt or attempt to quiet her. When she finally settled down and could speak normally again, she sniffed and asked, "May I use your handkerchief, please?"

"Sorry, I don't have one," Nick said. "But here, you can use my scarf. I don't mind."

The offer to use Nick's scarf to dry her eyes and blow her nose was so ridiculous and sweet all at once it caused Lucy to chuckle. "*Neh*, that's okay," she said, removing her mittens to dab her eyes with her bare fingers.

"I really am sorry," he repeated.

Lucy was embarrassed. "That's all right. I've stopped blubbering. I don't need a handkerchief after all."

"*Neh*, I mean I'm sorry I treated you in a way that made you feel…the way you feel. I didn't mean to. I was concerned. I care about you and I wouldn't want anything to happen to you. I especially wouldn't want to play a role in hurting you."

Lucy was overwhelmed by his words. No man had ever said anything like that to her before, even in friendship. "It's not your fault," she said. "And I do appreciate that you care. But I'm not as fragile as you think I am."

"Fragile? You? I don't think you're fragile at all, even if you are prone to pneumonia." Nick scoffed. "I think you're one of the most resilient women I've ever known."

Lucy was overwhelmed again. If this kept up, she was going to fall hard for Nick Burkholder. Maybe she already had.

LIEXP0919